Book Disclaimer

The works contained in this book are the result of many Free Write Fridays on the Clubhouse app. Hosted by David Lee Hawks and Hannah Bernadette Brennan, who have been faithfully gathering a small group of writers to create stories within a seven-minute timespan. The typical workflow is to open the room with a theme and get suggestions for prompts, based on that theme, from the writers in the room. So, depending on the number of people, the number of prompts can be anywhere from six to sixteen. The idea is to use a minimum of three prompts in the story about to be written, but if you can use all the prompts, you get bonus points and respect! The second prompt is chosen by David or Hannah, could be a theme or a word. If the room is going well, we will at times go for a third prompt. After writing the story in seven minutes, everyone takes turns reading their story aloud for the group to enjoy and make comments. Initially I was writing all of these stories in the Notes app of my Apple iPhone, but have also managed to type a few on my laptop, so some stories are a bit longer, based on the fact I was able to use a full keyboard instead of just my thumbs. I was urged by several members of the group to create this book based on regular positive reactions to my stories from everyone. Later on as the months progressed and Summer of 2022 arrived, covid restrictions were lessened and people began to do more things away from the computer. I hosted the group on my own for several months until everyone was too busy to keep it going. Special thanks to

Eric Cedeno for holding the last few sessions with me to hit 100 stories.

Story List

100 Stories
In
7 Minutes

By P. J. Galati

No, not That Cave
Prompt: an action sequence
Disclaimer: Both men have heavy Scottish accents.

Arnold observed the medium sized cave on the left.

"Are you sure this is the cave?" Arnold stared.

"Not really," Charlie dismally answered, "I was drunk!"

"You still are," Arnold pointed out.

"Whatever wizzy..." Charlie threw up his hands in exasperation.

Arnold rolled his eyes and entered the cave. It became dark after ten paces. He cast a luminous orb into being and gandered inside further.

"Are you coming?" Arnold asked as he looked back at the mouth of the cave and saw Charlie swaying a bit, but not stepping inside.

"Fuck that!" Charlie yelled, and the echo carried louder than Arnold had anticipated.

Deep in the darkness beyond the orb, a burst of flames shot outward, followed by a screechy roar. The Hellbender had been alerted and charged down the cave headed straight for Arnold, who braced himself for conflict with a freeze spell.

The Weird Diner
Prompt: eating dinner

Lowery felt weird. He'd been sitting there for at least thirty-seven minutes, doing his best not to fidget. He could feel the eyes on him...staring from pretty much everywhere in the diner. The environment was not one conducive to eating. Was it because he was human? The waitress had been ignoring him since he sat down despite his many attempts to get her attention? It's attention? Lowery could never tell the difference with Flickoneons. They had no obvious distinctions between their sexes. Why had he listened to Frank and come to this backwater diner on Kulvis?

"The food's good there," he'd said. "Almost like Martian food."

Lowery grimaced at the thought and looked over his shoulder...a rather mean looking Askonian was staring intently at him with six of his twelve eyes. Lowery slowly looked back in the direction of the server and finally made eye contact. Suddenly he heard the voice in his mind. "Human food?" It resounded. Lowery answered back vocally, "just give me the Special to go."

The bright blue Flickoneon nodded all its tentacles and looked at the chef through the order window, telepathically communicating his order. Lowery wondered if he'd get his food before someone shot at him or tried to swallow him whole.

Over Committed

Prompts: oath, sharing house, Netflix password, wedding bands

Jerry knew early on he was in over his head... he'd only been dating Elizabeth for two months and already they had a house together. It wasn't until he saw all her stuff, Jerry realized he had over committed. Elizabeth had seemed dark and sexy at first, but now it was obvious...she was a full-blown practicing witch. She'd moved into his house with all her crystals, skulls, brooms and even a jar of wedding bands! What was that about? Now she was sitting across from him... iPhone in hand... intently starring.

"Well?" She prompted.

"Huh?" Jerry replied.

"Didn't you hear me?" Elizabeth asked a bit irritated.

"I think I zoned out..." Jerry confessed.

"Look, you said we were committed... you took the house partner oath! I've heard a lot of excuses, but if you don't give me your Netflix password, we're gonna have a big problem tonight!"

Witch Way?

Prompt: lost in a hedge maze

Tim looked to the left...then to the right...or should he go straight? The hedges were at least twelve feet tall and he barely even saw sunlight, much less which direction the sun was in the sky. In other words, Tim was lost. He should have never agreed to meet Sharon in the center of the maze. What did he know about giant mazes? A sharp sound off to the left caught his attention, a rustling of underbrush. He ran left quickly, honing in on the noise. Turning a corner, Tim was confronted with a massive stone griffin. He stopped and starred at it.

"I don't suppose YOU know how to get to the center of this thing?" Tim asked sarcastically.

The griffin turned its head to look at Tim and a low rumbling growl escaped its mouth.

Tim's eyes went wide and he ran back the way he'd come. The griffin jumped down off its pedestal and chased after him, gaining ground thanks to its' four long lion legs.

"You have GOT to be kidding me here!" Tim yelled in horror.

Tim ran right into Sharon and they fell to the ground.

"Stop!" Sharon commanded.

The Griffin skidded to a grinding halt.

"As you wish, hedge witch," the griffin spoke.

"Are you okay?" Sharon asked Tim, who simply nodded, too stunned to answer.

Her Unspoken Promise
Prompt: A cabin in the woods

Billy tromped through the woods; his hand being tugged along by Katrina.

"Where are we going?" Billy asked with a curious smile.

"Somewhere that's worth it!" Katrina slyly implied.

Billy stared at her face until she faced forward again and then his gaze dropped to the most perfect bottom he'd ever grabbed before.

"We're here..." Katrina sang musically.

Billy looked up to see a log cabin that time forgot. It had to be four hundred years old.

"Here? That's where you wanna...do it?" Billy asked a little bashfully.

"Oh, you don't wanna?" Katrina said as she walked backwards towards the cabin, taking off her shirt and slowly unbuttoning her jeans.

Billy hurried after her, they both arrived at the door together and Katrina spun Billy around to face her, then opened the door and pushed Billy inside. He tripped and immediately fell into the gaping hole headed straight down into hell.

"I found another one master!" Katrina called out and slammed the door closed.

This Beach Sucks

Prompts: associated with the beach: sand, rain, garbage, sea glass, waves, sea life, Deadman's float, girls, hidden drinks, seagulls, sand scribble, sky, barefooted, cocktail, seashells

Christie stepped out of her car and flip-flopped her way across the parking lot until she hit the beginning of the beach. Kicking off her foot-ware, she dug here bare toes into the sand and stared up at the bright blue sky, listened to the waves, and took in a deep breath of fresh sea air. Then a seagull crapped on her favorite shirt.

"Are you kidding me bird?" She yelled.

Christie quickly tracked the bird and railed off a psychic dart which paralyzed the creature and it fell to the ground twitching.

Now she regretted listening to Franky... "go to the beach, there's plenty of hot girls there!" she mouthed sarcastically.

The words rang in her head as she scanned the area and pulled off her shirt to reveal her bikini top...might as well advise what these ladies would be getting. The place was littered with hot betties everywhere. Christie started stomping towards a black-haired beauty and hadn't made it more than five steps before stepping on an empty soda can which clamped around her right foot. "Fucking trash!" She stumbled sideways and then stepped on a crab which pinched her toes and she fell straight forward. Christie shot a burst of occult energy at both the attackers to her feet, knocking them loose. She looked in the direction of the beauty, who was now gone. The sun glinted off a piece of blue sea-glass right in front of her face just before the thunder clapped and it began to rain. She grabbed the sea-glass and stood up.

11

"Fuck this stupid beach" she huffed and stomped back to her car.

Bad Porn

Prompts: Things you find on the internet: rage, links, porn, lies, cute animals, wheelie shoes, YouTube, opinionated porn, viruses

Robert looked at Melissa's stern face and made his own.

"If you hadn't lied to me, we wouldn't be here, would we?" Melissa intoned.

"That's not really the point, you're just being difficult," Robert fussed.

"If it was normal porn or a regular link, I could click on web browser, right? That would be different!" She reminded him.

"Fine! I'll do it!" Robert yelled.

He pulled out a brass bowl, cut his hand with a ceremonial dagger to fill it, then chanted in a regular rhythm. He then dipped his fingers in the bowl and smeared the blood on his laptop, which caused it begin typing a web address in ancient cryptic text, which then sent them to www.risqueretroragerpornforwizards.wiz right away, a bizarre video began to play.

"You've got to be kidding me Robert?" Melissa was exasperated. "Actual dinosaur porn? Really? It's not like they're cute little animals!"

"Hey, you don't know if they did it or not!" He exclaimed.

"Yeah, but the lickalottapuss? You won't even go down.... Arrgggg.... We need to have a serious talk."

13

I'm Not that Pretty

Prompt: A memory that wasn't yours

Peter looked around the strange room. It had stone walls...he'd never been in...wait, was this a castle? Quickly scanning the room, he locked onto a set of large stained-glass doors that possibly led outside. He moved forward and suddenly felt this weird whooshing sensation, then stopped as he caught his reflection in a floor length mirror.

"What the bloody hell..." he spoke in a female voice.

Peter was dressed like a royal princess in a blue lacy gown, complete with busty female physique! He was a woman! A noise from outside brought his attention back to the doors, he rushed over and threw them open. The sight was pure shock. He was at the top of a castle spire, almost four hundred feet up! Nearly five seconds away from being snatched out of his princess room, by a giant golden dragon.

Peter was immediately kicked back into reality.

"Well? What did you find out Peter?" Beatrice asked intently.

"What the hell was that?" Peter asked confused.

"Oh my god...you were supposed to find out where the princess went! Do have any idea how hard it was to conjure that memory into you?" Beatrice intoned with frustration.

This Will End Badly

Prompts: (things in orbit) Mars, space junk, black hole, space station, George Clooney, moon, electron, Atlas, satellite, sun

Felicia stared out the porthole of the Mars Mark 7 Space Station at a piece of space junk.

"Come on!" She chanted.

"I'm telling you it's not gonna happen!" Gillian stared.

"It is so!" Felicia stated.

"You've got a higher chance of bringing George Clooney back from the dead." Gillian stated.

"You must be joking...he's been dead nearly 60 years...what's left to bring back?" Felicia looked at him, then back out at the space junk, just in time to see it smash into a satellite coming on an opposing orbit.

"Yes! I knew it! Pay up buster." Felicia demanded.

"Oh, I wasn't serious." Gillian stated.

"Is that so? Because I have it on this digital recorder and unless you want a trip to the moon prison colony, you better fork over those black hole thruster blueprints." Felicia glared.

"What about the electron discharge problem? That's still not solved!" Gillian stammered.

"What you mean is, YOU haven't solved it...but I have. Plans now or I'm gonna discharge you into the sun!"

Naughty Girl

Prompt: grounded

Lilly huffed and folded her arms, pouting as overtly as possible.

"Are you going to throw another tantrum?" Klem goaded her.

"Another tantrum? The last one was over a hundred years ago dad!" Lilly sneered.

"And your point…" Klem answered.

"The point? How long are you going to keep treating me like a little girl? I'm four hundred and seventy-seven years old!" Lilly stomped her foot to emphasize her point.

"And yet, you still managed to get caught feeding on a local boy… and you want to be treated better? Act your age, not like a rabid mongrel." Klem stared at her intently, his eyes piercing beyond her soul.

"I didn't ask to be born a vampire!" Lilly shouted.

"Look, you're grounded. No flying, no leaving the castle, and absolutely no Facebook, I'm sick and tired of getting those damned notifications!" Klem bared his fangs to make his point.

"Okay! Fine!" Lilly acquiesced. "Mother wouldn't be so strict." She mumbled.

"Oh yes? You want I should wake her up two decades early? For this nonsense? She'll REALLY love that!" Klem hissed.

"Fine! I'm gonna go finish my meal." Lilly started towards the door.

"No. I had Hildy take the boy back to the village. You're on rabbits for the next year." Klem informed her.

"Oh, please daddy no! Not rabbits! What about a few foxes? Maybe a bear or two?" Lilly pleaded, she locked eyes with her father and shriveled down into a tiny mouse and ran through a crack in the wall.

Deep Underground

Prompts: Things you do to waste time: Facebook, games, Netflix, procrastinate, talk to people, internet research, necking on/ snogging, thinking

Brinkle's eyes were bouncing back and forth between all the screens on his stone desk. The low light of the cave amplified a deep glow on his face with shifting colors. His hands moved quickly from keyboard to mouse, to touch pad to second mouse to custom joystick. Celia walked in his room and rolled her eyes.

"Brinkle! What are you doing?" She pestered him.

"What? What now? You know the rule, no sisters in my room!" Brinkle spat out in a kerfuffle.

"What do you mean, what? First off, I'm your only sister...You got Netflix open watching anime on one screen, yer playing a game on another, scoping out computer parts on Facebook marketplace and doing internet research on the internet? Who does that? You're not a human and even humans don't do this!" Celia insisted.

"I do it! That's who! I know I'm not human, you remind me daily, can you get out of my room?" Brinkle whined.

"Don't you want to like...talk to another troll, maybe a female to snog? Do you even think about these things?" Celia asked sarcastically.

"Yes! I know how to think! Now get your pestering gray and brown tale out of my cave!" Brinkle yelled and stared at her wild-eyed.

21

Feels So Good

Prompt: when it's really good, but also really bad

Priscila felt the breathing on her neck and shivered...

"Oh no," she whispered softly.

Her body began to tingle as she felt a light touch on her lower back which then traveled around her abdomen and to her inner thighs. The tingling became full waves of euphoria, pulsating through her system. She moaned and leaned into it. All her pleasure centers were registering a five-alarm fire which was on its way to seventeen.

"Why...why are you doing this to me..." she moaned.

Maximus kicked in the door and burst into the room, startling Priscila and the vampire feeding on her.

"Meal time's over you disgusting beast!" He yelled with rage.

Priscila twisted free and fell downward, a blade suddenly appearing in her hand, she drove the dagger straight through the vampires' foot, staking him to the wooden floor. Maximus charged with his teeth bared, "back to hell!"

Maximus grabbed the clawed appendage aimed for his face and drove his bare hand straight into the parasite's chest, twisting violently, he ripped its undead heart out and crushed it with a sickly disgust.

"Tell Satan my wife is off limits!"

Private Time

Prompt: something you should only have one of: toilet (commode), brain, mouth, robot, husband, biscuits or cookie, code.

Jerry gingerly placed his sizable buttocks squarely on the commode and opened the Sunday paper, searching intently for the comics section. A loud bang hit the bathroom door. "Every damn time," Jerry sighed.

"Master, I have procured your single cookie - bbbzzzrassppp- biscuit, as you requested." A female robotic voice said on the other side of the door.

"I asked you for that ten hours ago...last night! What is wrong with that mechanical brain of yours?" Jerry yelled.

"Do you not want to stick this dessert in your mouth hole any longer?" The robot continued.

"No!!! I'm on the damn toilet! What don't you understand about this?" Jerry yelled with irritation.

"I am -brrassasshhh- functioning properly husband." The female robot continued.

"We are not married!!" Jerry yelled.

"Why do you treat me this way? I am only trying to please you." The female robot continued.

"For the love of Christ, shut down code 84H5B." Jerry yelled.

"Why doooo....yyoouuuu....bbb rrrroooopppp." The robotic voice drifted off as she shut down.

"Finally..." Jerry sighed and went back to his comics, then he heard a plate with a cookie hit the floor and break. Jerry grimaced.

"For fucks sake." He rolled his eyes.

This is Awkward
Prompt: Love songs

Karen walked through the door and knew immediately; something was going on...Jason's apartment was clean...the lights were dimmed...she even smelled air freshener. She took off her coat and continued inside as Jason hurried past her into the kitchen. He began touching all the pots and pans that were cooking food, adjusting the oven, pulling out a bottle of wine, all in a rather unaccustomed fashion. The nail in the coffin was when he grabbed his phone, opened a playlist and love songs began to play on the apartment sound system, which was underpowered and staticky.

"Uhh... what's going on Jason?" Karen asked, inwardly hoping it wasn't what she feared.

"It's great right?" Jason smiled, "I figured it was time to go to the next level." He smiled as yet another sappy love song started.

"What level exactly? I'm only here because your sister said you needed help with your book..." Karen stated with trepidation.

"Oh, the book thing was a total lie... I knew you'd understand, you've been giving me all those signals at the BBQ's...." He smiled.

"No Jason...I'm allergic to your dad's dog...and the other weekend I had food poisoning." She relayed.

"Oh....oh shit." Jason grimaced.

I Should Have Known

Prompt: pettifoggery, pettifogger

Leslie stared at the man in front of her. His cowboy duster looked like it had died several years ago, but the man had refused to accept this fundamental fact.

"Well, what's it gonna be darlin?" Butch asked.

"I'm not sure you're the lawyer for me..." Leslie said with trepidation.

"Yain't gonna find a gooder one round here!" Butch stated emphatically.

"Look, Butch....this isn't a simple matter of pettifoggery...my land is overrun by chupacabras and neither the sheriff, nor the town are willing to do something about it...you really think you're the man to file the appropriate papers to get some traction?" She stared intently.

"Well shit darlin, hain't no need fer papers! I got a twelve gauge in ma truck! I'll take care'a dem bastards real gud!" Butch rambled happily.

Dirt Sandwich

Prompt: Things associated with Recess: Dodgeball,
Playground, Double Dutch, Crowd, Monkey Bars, Bullies,
Dirt, Darkness, Breather, Sandbox, Purity, Loneliness,
Swings, Noise, TJ

Talula stared out onto the playground and carefully scanned the noisy crowd, trying to find her target. The monkey bars were occupied by a group of Ding-Bats, she always thought that was such a stupid name. A group of Jingle Clowns were jumping double Dutch on the dodgeball court, drawing the usual crowd of gawkers with their ridiculous cacophony of bells. A black and orange streak across the yard caught her attention, Jerry the Fox-Lark half ran then flew straight into the quadruple swing set, trying his hardest to flip the swing 360 degrees, but as usual, stalled at the top, fell and had to quickly recover before hitting the swing bar. He rebounded off, semi controlled with a bit of wing and fox tail action, unfortunately, he lost his balance and went head first into the sandbox. Which was where Huxby happened to be doing his best to hide. Talula took off running and pounced on Huxby.

"Thought you could hide from me?" Talula beamed.

"Leave me alone!" Huxby squirmed.

"Hey Talula, why do you have to be such a bully all the time?" Jerry the Fox-Lark starred as he sat up, shaking the sand out of his large pointed ears.

"Mind your own business Fox boy. I know you can't stand anyone who isn't full of purity like you, but you interrupt me again and I'll stuff your head so far down in that sand you'll be breathing darkness for a month! Then you'll really know what loneliness is!" Talula yelled.

"Such a mouth breather." Jerry huffed, ruffled his feathers and left.

"I don't want to eat a dirt sandwich!" Huxby squealed.

Talula pinned him further into the sand.

"I bet you don't..." Talula smiled and kissed Huxby right on the lips.

"TJ, you could have just kissed me to start," Huxby smirked.

"What fun would that be?" She teased.

Undeath is Unfair

Prompt: Sunshine
Disclaimer: The entire family is British, read with a
cockney accent

Clair looked out the window and sighed heavily. It was a bright day, full of sunshine, lush greenery and a gentle breeze, the hot light on her pale cheeks.

"Mum! She's staring out the window again! Make her stop!" Bruno yelled.

Clair's mum rushed into the room.

"Clair, you need to pull down the shade, you know the rules!" Her mum chastised.

"It's not my fault you know!" Clair fussed.

"That's no excuse and you know it, Sunshine!" Bruno taunted.

"Stop calling me that!" Clair yelled back.

"Then stop sitting in the sunlight!" Bruno spat out.

"Clair, we're all vampires, you too," her mother reminded, "just because you were born with a deformity, you shouldn't taunt your brother, you know he'll catch fire."

"I'm not deformed!" Clair screamed.

"Then why doesn't the sunlight burn you?" Bruno yelled. "You are a freak and you know it!"

"Bruno, don't talk to your baby sister that way." Their mother commanded.

"I'm not a baby either!" Clair whined, "I'm 78 years old mummy, when are you going to start treating me that way!"

"Wait till your father gets here, you can take it up with him. I'm finished dealing with you." Her mother said with disgust.

"I wish you were dead!" Bruno yelled.

33

"We're all undead you twat!" Clair rolled her eyes, and went back to staring out the window.

A Night at the Theater

Prompt: The Theater of the Absurd
Disclaimer: Nissa is British, read her lines with a Cockney
accent. Also, this story after being read aloud, was
requested for further writing so it is double the normal
length of writing time.

Carl stared at Nissa with a blank face. She stared
back and shrugged her shoulders. The large wooden
double doors buckled and bounced behind them.

"We can't stay here," Nissa said in a low voice.

Carl made a snap decision, ran over to the ticket
line for the theater and grabbed two of the large rope
dividers between some brass poles. He ran back to Nissa
and together they secured the doors. Carl grabbed her
hand and they ran up to the second floor, then into the
plush main office, which was empty. After locking and
securing the door with a large highbacked leather chair,
Nissa looked out the window while Carl brought up the
video security feed on the office computer.

"Carl...it's bad outside..." Nissa drifted.

"The same as in here?" Carl asked.

Nissa looked at the security feeds, inside the giant
theater, about three hundred plus well-dressed zombies
were slowly mulling around, even the ice skaters in the
middle rink were staggering and sliding oddly. Carl looked
outside the window and saw a similar scene.

"We're trapped in here," Carl admitted, and turned
to look at Nissa.

"I've always fancied you," Nissa confessed, then
slammed her body into Carl, her hands groped him
hungrily and her mouth quickly found his, tongues locked,
they both dropped to the floor as heavy breathing ensued.

35

"Get this shirt off!" Carl breathed, which Nissa was only too happy to rip off, followed by her own.

"You're so fit!" Nissa eyed him like a plate of chocolate brownies, then went to work on his slacks. Carl suddenly felt like he was being attacked by a really hot, sexy shark, ferociously and hungrily trying to get at his bare flesh. Almost both completely naked, fully engrossed in one another, a side door in the office opened suddenly, catching both lovers off guard. In staggered a zombie dressed as Abraham Lincoln. Carl rolled quickly up off the floor, looked wildly around the room and grabbed a floor standing American flag pole with a spear pointed eagle at the tip, then charged the zombie, impaled it and shoved the creature straight out the open window, down to the street below. He then quickly closed the side door and locked it, sharply turning to face Nissa.

"You're so fucking lush!" Nissa lunged for him.

"Lush?" Carl asked.

"Yeah, Lush! Fuck'n Tidy! Let's snog you cheeky bastard!" Nissa said as she jumped on Carl, wrapped her legs around him and rode her sexy beast to the floor.

Someone's In Trouble

Prompts: A monologue by one person AND/OR Winter
Sports

Harold paced back and forth, side eyeing the room. The smell of wet wood and a crisp hot fire filled the entire space. Twelve sets of eyes tracked his movement as he continued to mull over his thoughts and crossed paths with the fireplace, which caused shadows to jump around the room since it was the only source of light. Harold finally stopped and looked at the group.

"I'm really struggling to understand this...this entire....who thought this was a good idea?" Harold looked at everyone single person in the room one at a time. A few of them squirmed, but said nothing.

"I mean, I'm all for innovations and anything that you guys think might spice things up.... but this is a bobsled team... BOB....SLED.... in no way possible would it have..... no competition would..... where did you guys get the jet turbines from? Seriously? You can't just go anywhere....." Harold stopped for a moment when it looked like Melissa was going to say something, but apparently she was just shifting in her seat.

"I'm sure it made the sled feel really fast, but you're lucky no one died! And who is gonna pay for Mrs. Jenkins shed? And the repairs to sled number three? I'm very disappointed in all of you! I have no idea how whoever was in the sled jumped clear.... but I'm going to find out.... and whoever it was... no hot coco for the rest of the season!"

37

Kilenger Went Down

Prompts: Comedic duo interaction or I went to a funeral today and this was so funny.
Disclaimer: Harvey has a gruff voice, Tabetha has a Cockney British accent

The group gathered around the grave was medium in size. Harvey stood next to Tabetha in full battle armor, with the traditional black and red torn strips of material required by the guild at such events. The irony of a necromancer performing the funeral rites was not lost on either of them.

"Kilenger went down hard," Harvey said somberly.

"Kilenger was a bloody idiot with no sense of direction or timing!" Tabetha spat out.

"Shhhhh!" Nabby the dwarf eyed them meanly. "Show some respect."

"Sod off Nabby, ya twit," Tabetha spat back.

"I mean, he wasn't really the best hunter in the clan," Harvey admitted.

"Not the best?" Tabetha was awestruck. "He was killed by a blue squirrel!"

"Yeah, but did you see the size of that squirrel?" Harvey's eyebrows rose as he spoke to emphasize his point.

"Yeah....I seen bigga (sniff) he was a dink 'en ya know it..." Tabetha grimaced.

"I tol ya SSSHHH!" Nabby said again and stared them both down for a long moment before facing forward again.

Tabetha gently elbowed Harvey with and evil smile, then firmly placed her right boot on Nabby's back and shoved him head first right into the open grave, then they both laughed hysterically.

Oasis in the Valley

Prompts: (Something Simple) Being Still, Driving, Simple
Syrup, Ice cream, Bugs, Breathing, Honesty, Oatmeal,
Sleeping, Laughing, Thinking
Disclaimer: Both women have Valley Girl accents

Candy and Crystal entered the Dessert-o-rama and were blasted with frosty cool air that reeked of simple syrup. The gaudy bright colors splattered around the place were all competing for their eyes to follow.

"Oh, my-gawd...I cannot believe you were driving-around-in-circles to bring me here..." Crystal said as she rolled her eyes.

"Honestly, I knew if I told you, ugh, the huffy breathing and girl, you are always thinking too much." Candy answered and stared her dead in the eye.

"Am I supposed to be all happy and giggly? Laughing about how you managed an illusion spell without me noticing? I am not in the mood Candy," Crystal relayed sarcastically.

"Oh I'm sorry, would you rather be sleeping under a tree, inhaling all the bugs within like, everywhere around....or come here and get some oatmeal ice cream!" Candy's eyes were gigantic with the mention of a seemingly sweet yet healthy dessert.

"Oh please, just stand there and be still while I gather myself...I need to prepare...this is not the kind of witchy work I thought we'd be doing today." Crystal stated as she fanned her face with both hands.

"Fine, ice cream first, then we can conjure that money demon you've been pestering me about!" Candy teased.

"Oh-my-gawd! It's not a money demon, that was so last season, I need a cash faerie or a profit pixie!" Crystal rolled her eyes.

Wet Terror

Prompt: Running From
Disclaimer: listen to this music while reading on
youtube.com/watch?v=EiR3PGAYhF4 - Nature Boy
Instrumental - Moulin Rouge! Original Score

Goliath was running so fast, the trees were a blur around him. Silvia was barely able to keep up with the fit quadrupede. They both breathed heavily, the sound of wet, rapid, sloppy footfalls behind them closing in fast. Goliath tripped on a branch and took a muzzle full of dirt and leaves, which he quickly shook off and recovered to continue running. Silvia quickly searched her mind and her training for anything that would help her in this situation. She instinctively grabbed for her fanny pack with her knife inside, only to find it missing. What had her master been telling her for so long?

"The enemy is a shapeless terror which will eventually overcome you...so be ready."

The squishy sounds of the creature got closer, she dared not chance a look back, for fear of being nailed in the face by a low branch. The forest was starting to dim, right in the middle of the day...this shouldn't be happening...why hadn't she listened to her sister and gone for a movie instead. Silvia could feel the creature behind her...nearly upon her...then suddenly it stopped. Goliath stopped short and Silvia nearly ran right over a cliff, but caught a tree at the last moment. She spun around quickly, grabbed a branch and a rock off the ground.

"Come on your bastard!" Silvia shouted.

Goliath stood next to Silvia and growled.

Slowly a shape lumbered towards them, then leaned on a tree, breathing hard. It came closer, out of the shadows, into the light...it was...a wet man.

"What do you want!" Silvia yelled.

"What do I want? Lady...what the hell is wrong with you? You dropped this off the bridge and hit me in the face with it, I fell right in the lake...been trying to give it back to you....I've been chasing you for ten minutes!" He said, exasperated and out of breath.

"Oh...um.. thank you?" Silvia said uncertainly and took the fanny pack from him.

"You're welcome," the man said and straightened up, wiped his wet brow and smiled at her.

Goliath growled loudly and barked. A giant blurry shadow appeared out of nothingness, tackled the man and took him right over the cliff.

Pierce Me

Prompts: From the point of view of a body part (Neck bitten by a vampire)

It was just a normal night at first...how I love the cool wind, it cascades off the small hairs I have, not like those massively thick hairs on the head, my neck hairs were fine and silken...like royalty. I could feel the moonlight pulsating against me like a distant pressure. While I couldn't sense the darkness, I intuitively knew it...plus I got a b-mail from the eyes and the nose, they are always telling me the body's business.

These night walks are...whoa...what's happening...the equilibrium shifted rapidly...there's a body wide alert...there's....sudden pain! I'm being pierced! I'm being attacked! Something is on me! I'm bleeding, my life force is...oh...ooohhhh....oh my....what is that sensation...is that....euphoria? The alert is all wavy now...I feel...warm and gooey. What is this wet hotness...something is inside me....it's invading me...I feel virginal...oh yes...yes more....it stopped...the heat is....I'm losing the sensation...I can't hold on to it...the body is slowing down...I feel so lost...why hath thee abandoned me....

Rumored Treasure

Prompts: Things that make you go oowww: Something
Shiny, Jazz, New Discovery, Visible Panty-lines under
leggings at the gym, Mud, Worts, Stubbing your toe

Bobby carefully picked his way through the forest
underbrush as quietly as possible; he had some suspicions
about where he was headed, but really couldn't be certain.
It was akin to searching for buried treasure on the
strength of a rumor as to the location...but a new
discovery, that's what kept him going. He could tell the
water was close. Bobby parted a thick bush just in time to
see Susan take off her shirt. She was still wearing those
tight leggings women loved to wear at the gym, he could
see her panty-line from where he stood. Then just like
that, the leggings and panties were gone and her shiny
smooth butt was greeting him with a sideways grin.

"Are you just gonna stand there all creepy-like in
the bushes?" Susan called out as she turned her head in his
direction.

Bobby pushed through the bushes, stubbed his toe
on a rock and tripped, falling face first into a mud puddle
which was hidden by some leaves.

"Bobby! Is that you?" Susan squealed and quickly
covered her naked bits.

Bobby raised his face, it had chunks of mud
covering it, he looked like he'd contracted some kind of
rapid wort's disease.

"Yup, it's me." Bobby blurbed.

"How did you find me?" She demanded.

"Jazzy Joe told me you like to skinny dip..." Bobby
confessed as he got up and wiped off his face.

47

"That big mouthed bastard!" Susan yelled, then signed...."Fine, you better get naked, if you wanna play," She smiled deviously, then sauntered over to the water and entered the lake like it was made of sex lube.

The Chosen One
Prompts: Natural Selection

Nevel stood stock still, pondering the events that had led him to this exact moment. He wondered if any of the others were also perusing the rolodex of their lives. Kleo had so much sweat pouring down her face, it looked like she was crying...or she may have also been crying...but silent tears were a rarity for her. Glancing sideways to Frankford, the big man looked angry and terrified at the same time, but he dared not move a muscle.

The seven-foot-tall Vilifier loomed in front of them, taking deep sniffing whiffs of the group. Nevel couldn't see the rest of the people in the camp without moving, but he assumed they too were aware that death was waiting for someone. Vilifiers would only eat someone if they carried a specific DNA sequence, but there was no way to know which one it was looking for tonight. Different breeds sniffed for different DNA. It had started at the far right of the group, and was making its way down towards Nevel. Everyone knew it would kill you just the same if it viewed you as a threat. The overly thin, stringy scaled body looked like a caricature of a monster, but all the spikes and large fangs exiting both feral heads were overly terrifying. Nevel continued to watch the creature with his peripheral vision as it went down the line, searching for its next meal.

Just as his master had taught him for situations like this one, Nevel calmed his breathing, and focused his energy. The Vilifier was only one person away, it was time to take a risk and mask himself. Invisible to everyone, Nevel was now undetectable to most natural probing. The Vilifier moved from Kleo to him and almost moved right to Frankford, but caught itself and paused, taking a whiff with only one head. Nevel took this to mean the masking had indeed worked, it only detected him visually, and nearly missed him all together. Nevel relaxed for a brief moment and got ready. The creature moved on to fully put both heads in front of Frankford. As if choreographed for effect, both heads began to bare fangs, mouths open wide, Frankford had the DNA it wanted, it was now or never.

Nevel loosed the Ethereal sword from its spectral sheath hidden in his right arm. He sprang forward to the left, severing the Vilifiers left leg off at the knee. It was critical to bring the heads lower, no amount of lower body damage would kill it. Nevel dove and rolled tightly, spinning upwards and ready. The enraged beast twisted its body as it fell, becoming a three-legged creature with just the one leg and two twangy clawed arms. It charged Nevel. He dove left and cleaved right with his Ethereal sword, avoiding the second head as he sliced the first one in half. He again rolled tightly and sprang up, anticipating the attack which was coming. Suddenly, out of nowhere, Kleo appeared in the air, mid-leap, she brought a large axe straight down on the remaining head, but it caught on one of the larger rear spikes. Nevel leapt forward, and forced his sword straight through the left eye socket to finished the Vilifier off before it could turn on Kleo and rip her in half. She managed to avoid all the head spikes by using the axe handle as a pole to push off of and she rolled to the side, landing a bit ungracefully. Nevel walked over and offered his hand to help her up. She took it and breathed in deeply as she rose, as if to inflate herself back into a fully living woman, steadying her body.

"Why didn't you tell us you were a Soul Reaper?" Kleo smiled with relief.

The Proper Barnacular

Prompts: The Cat Meowed, Aliens love dogs, could be worse, I am she, let me think, stop right/write now, street is wet, looking down further, its Halloween witch, horse eats ice cream, life goes on
Disclaimer: Charlie has a British Accent

Charlie looked at his dismal surroundings and realized...it could be worse. A burned down barn offered very little in the way of cover, but when the street is wet, he did what he could to stay dry. He hated being in these situations.

"Come on Charlie, pull it together man." He mumbled to himself.

"What are you doing here?" A voice boomed through the half open space.

"Who is that?" Charlie stood up quickly.

"Stop right now!" The voice commanded and Charlie froze in place.

"Where are you?" Charlie asked, obviously nervous.

"I'm down here." The loud female voice said.

Charlie looked around the barn, but only saw mud, hay and rusty old farm equipment.

"Down where?" Charlie asked.

"Straight down." She intoned.

Charlie looked down and the floor, then...looking down further, he spotted the tiniest person he'd ever seen. She looked like an action figure toy, nearly six inches tall. she was dressed in rags and carried a small stick. No wonder she wanted him to stop, he'd nearly stepped on her.

"Who are you?" Charlie asked as he crouched down closer to her.

"I'm Zelda the Witch!" Zelda announced forcefully.

"Really?" Charlie asked with disbelief.

"Yes really! What's your name giant!" She asked.

"Oh...um, I'm Charlie." He answered.

"Oh really? Are you sure your names Charlie?" She asked sarcastically.

Charlie was of course chagrined. A bit of motion drew Charlie's attention to the broken door where a cat was silhouetted. It stared with glowing eyes, the cat meowed and then ducked back outside.

"What day is it giant Charlie?" Zelda asked.

"It's Halloween witch!" Charlie said emphatically.

"I thought as much...lost my cellphone..." Zelda mumbled.

"Are you sure you're Zelda the witch?" Charlie stared.

"Indeed, I am she!" Zelda commanded with pride. "Have you ever seen a horse eat ice cream?"

"Let me think...uhh... no... should I have?" Charlie asked.

"Well....I have, but I'm rather well traveled." She replied matter-of-factly.

"Oh really? Did you know aliens love dogs?" Charlie asked.

"Pssshhh, who doesn't know that?" Zelda rolled her eyes.

"I really need to get going Zelda," Charlie stood up.

"Yeah, yeah, life goes on...go tromp somewhere else giant Charlie." Zelda said with a wave of her hand and disappeared before his eyes.

The Wrong Left

Prompts: The road less taken
Disclaimer: both characters are Irish

Evergreen trees were swiftly disappearing as Valerie ran full out, her entire bare body was drenched in sweat. Next to her, O'Leary was struggling to keep up, but had managed to at least retain his shorts.

"I can't keep this up!" O'Leary breathed heavily.

"Wanna stop? You go right on ya wanker!" Valerie audaciously retorted.

"Yeah, sod off, it'll be gone by now..." O'Leary reassured.

"That so? Oh, well then, go on, have a picnic!" Valerie rolled her eyes and pushed forward.

She came up short right as O'Leary was looking over his shoulder and he ran right into her. She tripped forward, then turned around and smacked him across the face.

"You try'n to cop a feel, ya prick?" Valerie asked angrily.

"Owww! I were look'n behind ya daft wench!" O'Leary answered as he rubbed his face. "Why'd you stop?"

Valerie displayed with both hands, like she was Vanna White on that American game show, a split in the dirt road. The left path looked raw and nearly invisible with overgrowth.

"Let's take that one," O'Leary pointed to the left.

"Yeah, you still got shorts on, them trees are gonna tear me up!" Valerie said as she rubbed her bare skin.

"Really yeah? Then why ya ask me?" O'Leary intoned bitterly. A roar off in the distance turned both their heads to reveal the four-meter-tall werewolf was still chasing them.

It's Possessed

Prompts: (Rock and Roll) Drugs, trains and throwing TVs
out windows

Harvey stared at his band mates Duke and Leo. He
blinked his eyes several times as if trying to clear blurry
vision. He looked out the train window at the countryside
passing by.

"Nope, I got nuthin," Harvey said lazily.

"I told ya ta take more than that, more LSD is
always the way to go bro!" Duke said as he demonstrated
some invisible equation in the air with his hands.

"I gave him the right amount dude!" Leo insisted.

"Then why ain't nuthin happen'n?" Duke asked.

"Hey, can you guys change the TV channel?"
Harvey asked.
Duke and Leo looked behind them at the TV, which was
blank.

"It's definitely working," Duke and Leo said
simultaneously.

"Thanks guys. OH! Man this one is worse! Way
worse! Holy shit! The devil is selling my soul on a used
souls lot! Guys, we gotta buy my soul back! Who has a
credit card?" Harvey yelled.

"There's no devil bro!" Duke yelled.

Harvey jumped up, ripped the TV off its shelf,
kicked out the train window and then forced the TV out
the hole.

"Shit man, why'd you do that?" Leo asked.

"The devil was eating my soul with hot sauce
because no one was bidding on it!" Harvey yelled.

"How is throwing the TV out the window gonna stop him from eating it?" Duke asked.

"Oh…uh…it made sense at the time…" Harvey somberly admitted.

Rock Out

Prompts: Sex, Drugs, Rock and Roll
Disclaimer: Both people are Indian, living in the United
States.

Mustafa listened to Guns and Roses playing in the background as he twisted his thick mustache and eyed Hilatia. She was unconsciously swaying to the music, her hips drawing his attention. He allowed a smile to creep over his face. He looked at the bowl of M&M's next to him, imagined it was actually illegal drugs that rock and rollers would eat like candy...even though this was actually candy...he grabbed a handful and shoved it in his mouth, chewing loudly, reveling in the crunchy sounds as a third of them fell on the floor and raced away.

Mustafa bounced up out of his chair and began to move his hips in the same rhythm with Hilatia. He imagined the two of them bumping and grinding together, rocking out into the night. She was so smoking hot. He stared at her as he reached for the bowl of M&M's again and clipped the edge, knocked it over and sent its contents straight to the floor. The bowl broke into several pieces.

"Ah crap." Mustafa's mood was totally disrupted.

Hilatia, looked across the second-floor alleyway to Mustafa's building.

"Are you okay?" She asked.

Mustafa looked up, slightly embarrassed.

"Oh, yes. I am fine. Thank you." Mustafa answered.

Hilatia nodded, and went back to dancing in her apartment.

Mustafa sank back into his seat, feeling dejected and staring at his spoiled candy drugs all over the floor.

A Safe Place

Prompts: Things that creep or crawl - skin, zombies,
spider, regrets, black widow, caterpillar, thoughts

Frederick took a slow deep breath in and released it
the same way, like he was smoking a cigar and blowing out
the smoke. The unpainted bare-wood-board room made
him feel like he was somewhere in the Old West, some
abandoned ghost town building...but he was in northern
New Jersey. The second floor had seemed like a safe choice
to hide at the time, but now he was beginning to regret his
decision. Frederick looked out the cracked window and
saw no fewer than seven zombies creeping around outside
in the overgrown grass. A spider slid down on its silk
strand right in front of his face, which made him jump
back.

"Another spider?" Alicia asked offhandedly.

'Yes-another-one!" Frederick spat out. "This place
is infested!"

"Was it a black widow?" Alicia continued
nonchalantly.

"No. Just one of those fat garden spiders," he
answered after rifling through his thoughts, trying to
identify which species it happened to be.

"You have the be the jumpiest guy I know." She
continued.

"How many guys you know are left?" Frederick
raised an eyebrow.

"I bet you would totally freak if a cute little
caterpillar was on you," She commented.

"I don't like crawly things on my skin!" Frederick
snapped, then caught himself and glanced out the window
again to check if the zombies heard him.

59

"Ya, I got that. Listen, are you gonna keep me tied up?" Alicia stared and struggled against her bound arms and legs.

"Are you gonna try to fuck me again?" Frederick stared back.

"I mean, I might...I'm super horny." She smirked deviously.

Witch Dessert

Prompts: A difficult decision

Vera sighed heavily and looked out at the dessert table. There were so many choices, but where to start. Her mother wouldn't allow such a spread, but Vera was a full-grown witch and she did what she wanted, no matter what her mother thought.

She eyed the brownies, then lingered on the chocolate cake a bit too long before passing right over a bowl of sour gummy bears.

"I should have gone for more variety," she mumbled.

Vera looked at the other end of the table, a bowl of candied apples, a plate of cannoli's, a melty bowl of double fudge brownie ice cream...and the rest of the table was taken up by Ted. She lingered on Ted long enough that it appeared as though her decision had been made.

"Oh Ted, you do look rather yummy," she smiled at him and removed his gag.

"Listen lady, I'm really not into whatever the hell this is right here, okay?" Ted rambled nervously.

"Oh, is that so?" Vera raised an eyebrow and stuck the gag back in his mouth.

This caused him to shake his head and try to speak, so she removed the gag.

"What is it now Ted?" Vera patiently asked.

"Why am I naked and how come I can't move?" Ted asked.

"Well, you can't move because I've enchanted you. As for the nudity...so I can see what part of you I want." Vera smiled.

"Oh," Ted laughed nervously, "I uh, I was thinking bad thoughts."

"I'm sure you were, but I think I've made my decision...it was rather difficult." Vera smiled, then re-gaged Ted. She picked up a large sacrificial Damascus dagger and three tined fork, which she then sank right into Teds right thigh and began slicing. Ted tried to scream, but it came out muffled by the gag.

"I know, I know Ted, I'm a thigh girl," Vera smiled hungrily, "the tastiest part!"

Lock Stock Diva

Prompts: Don't put that in there / That doesn't go there

Lola snuggled into Clive, pressing her body against his, her soft bits fitting in between his hard parts. She stretched her neck and nibbled his ear, then slyly slid her tongue in, which got him to pull away quickly and he immediately   wiggled his ear out with his finger and threw her off of him.

"Ug, you know I can't stand that!" Clive whined. "Tongues don't belong in ears!"

"So you keep telling me," Lola smiled and climbed on top of him.

"And yet, you never seem to recall it..." Clive said and grabbed her thighs, then rolled her over so he was on top.

"I have a hearing problem," Lola pouted. "Didn't you say you wanted to put something of yours where it didn't belong?" She smirked and wiggled her butt.

"I said no such thing," Clive smiled, "it seems like you want something somewhere..."

"Do you promise to give it to me?" Lola pursed her lips.

"Oh yeah!" Clive smiled, and moved up off Lola enough for her to flip over and exposed her naked bottom.

"Here it comes," Clive warned her, then grabbed a plush teddy bear on the other side of the bed and shoved it head first into her butt, wiggling it crazily. Lola screamed and laughed wildly bucked all over the place.

"You fuzzy devil!" She squealed.

My Girl

Prompts: Things we never regret: authenticity, laughter, chocolate, True Love, contraception, a good time

Kline looked at Tootie, who looked back with authenticity born of selfless true love. They were out for a walk after dinner, it was their usual routine. It was such a simple thing, but it was honest and good exercise. Kline snuck a glance at his cellphone to see how much longer the sun would be up. Walking in the dark made Tootie a little nervous and Kline liked to take care of her as best he could. They'd been introduced four years ago and as soon as he saw her beautiful chocolate fur, he knew she was the Australian cattle dog for him. Plus, she jumped all over him immediately. Kline had never regretted his decision.

"You having a good time girl?" Kline looked down at her.

Tootie wagged her tail and panted, then sneezed in response. Kline was lucky, most of the litter had already been adopted. It was so different for dogs than it was for people. Dogs didn't use contraception, and from what he could tell, didn't really have the same hang-ups over pups as humans did over their kids.

Deciding to get a dog right after his wife had died during childbirth was a risk. Many people warned him against it, telling him he would indeed regret trying to replace his wife and child with a dog, but they had all been wrong. Tootie reminded him of Melissa in so many ways. She was always there for him, always happy to see him and loved to snuggle. His life was still full of laughter and fun pranks thanks to this faithful companion.

Birkey Ain't Mad
Prompts: Laughing Too Hard

This day had not started off how it ended up. Birkey was so excited to get his tattoo. He was a rather larger man, who could easily be mistaken for one of those Harley Davison biker dudes. All he needed was a bandana on his scalp and a leather cut around his shoulders. Today was the day he was moving forward, starting a new chapter of his life and this tattoo was a symbol of that choice. Once it was done, he looked and his eyes were transfixed. He couldn't look away for a full two minutes. The Tattoo artist stared at him.

"You okay bruh?" He asked.

Birkey smiled and began laughing and he didn't stop. He was laughing too hard. It wasn't forced, it was more of a mania...the type of laugh you hear from a truly insane person. The kind of laugh that sends chills up your spine and makes you want to slowly or rapidly edge away from the person who's creating it.

Birkey jumped out of the tattoo chair, grabbed the tattoo artist by the throat with one meaty, massive paw and rode him straight to the floor. He smiled crazily as he continued laughing and turned his free hand into a ham-fist which he used to beat the life out of his victim. The tattoo artist squirmed and his arms flailed all over the place as he struggled, but there was no way for him to push off the mountain that was now on top of him. The commotion drew attention from the other end of the shop and Lilly the front desk girl came running back.

"What the hell are you doing!" Lilly yelled.

Birkey stopped laughing and hitting the man simultaneously, then craned his head with resistance as if it moved on rusty gears and looked at Lilly.

"Tell me what the tattoo says..." Birkey commanded in a gravelly voice.

Lilly looked on his arm at the heart shaped tattoo with a banner on it and gasped.

"Read it!" Birkey commanded again.

"Um...No Regerts," Lilly timidly read.

"Exactly!" Birkey growled, "No Regerts!"

Birkey then ratcheted his head back towards his punching sack.

"You're gonna regert today bruh!" Birkey grimaced and resumed beating the man.

Witch Doctor

Prompts: Tools - claw hammer, needle nose pliers, axe, crowbar, tweezer, screw driver, cordless drill, scissors
Disclaimer: Witch Doctor speaks with a Jamaican accent

Clair was extremely worried about her decision to listen to the locals on an impulse. Their rental car had blown a tire and they careened off the road right into a ditch which flipped them over twice. Jerry had been badly wounded, but she came away nearly unscathed. There was no hospital nearby in this part of Jamaica, the locals had directed her to a witch doctor, who was the only person in the village that could possibly help, or so she hoped. They'd brought Jerry in on a stretcher made of freshly cut young trees and bound together with vines.

Upon entering the witch doctors hut, she was surprised by what she saw. Hanging on the wall were several tools, a claw hammer, axe, crowbar, needle nose pliers, screwdrivers, all the sort of things you would see in a garage workshop, not in a place that does surgery.

"Well now, dis mon be suf'rin. I got to op'rate straight away," the witch doctor candidly informed her.

Jerry was laid on a table and he took out a pair of scissors, quickly cutting off all her husband's clothes to get a better look at his body. The witch doctor then jumped up on the table like a spider monkey and examined Jerry all over.

A cordless drill suddenly appeared in his hand and he immediately drilled right into Jerry's chest, blood spurted from the wound. Clair covered her mouth to stop from screaming. He then put down the drill and picked up a set of tweezers, which he shoved into the newly drilled hole and twisted it around until he found something and then slowly pulled out a small shard of glass. Jerry sat bolt

69

up with a deep breath in and then swayed a bit. The witch doctor caught him just before Jerry fell sideways.

"Dis man wore cursed!" The witch doctor exclaimed.

"What are you talking about?" Clair asked wide eyed. "What was that you pulled out of him?"

"Dat be cursed sea glass. An-noda witch try'n ta kill ya two. Tis a salty curse." He informed her. "Wur did he drink last?"

"We just had something to eat at a friend's house two villages away." Clair spoke with dread.

"Dem people not be yer friends." The witch doctor stared into her eyes which made her feel more angry than uncomfortable.

Back Again

Prompts: Teamwork

While Lucas was not a poster boy for teamwork, it was part of his job to lead. After being reincarnated four hundred and thirty-seven times, he knew his duty as a Centurion Maji and a general in the Atlantian military, was to follow orders. Even if those directives were over ten thousand years old. Rishi was the only other Centurion Maji he'd been able to locate in this lifetime, but that didn't bother him much. Some of the other magi under his command took issue with his leadership style. Rishi shared the same ideals and a complementary skillset to his own. The alarming absence of were-creatures in this present time was a clear symptom of why the current situation was spiraling out of control.

They'd been in Brooklyn for the last two years, handling the temporary vampires which kept popping up all over the five boroughs of New York. It was obvious to Lucas, an original was at the center of it. They'd been searching for months until he'd spotted Emuishéré with her daughter Shamisé at a night club, working some tourists. Lucas and Rishi began formulating a plan on how to deal with such a powerful adversary. It wasn't until tonight though, they discovered the mansion in Brooklyn, led by Emuishéré, full of married vampire couples. They were far away from the great war with Lemoria, but his directive was clear...all their super soldiers, the vampires, were to be removed in this life or the next.

Danger Fruit

Prompts: Types of fruits or vegetables - Tomato, lemon,
papaya, strawberries, apricots, cucumber, dragon fruit,
asparagus, Brussels sprouts, apple
Disclaimer: Matilda and Jeremy are southerners with
thick accents

Jeremy shuffled down the hall with his apple,
strawberry and lemon smoothie in hand. He took a swig
and immediately regretted it, spitting the contents onto
the floor.

"What the shit...." he mumbled under his breath.

Jeremy turned on his heel and strode back into the
kitchen where Matilda was smiling evilly.

"You did that on purpose didn't ya? Ya wretched
witch!" Jeremy shouted.

"That's right ya stupid bastard!" Matilda sneered,
then lobbed a dragon fruit right at his head.

Jeremy dodged the fruit but didn't look behind
him until the tiny dragon had already burst out of its fruit
shell and began attacking his head.

"You dirty wench!" He cried as he fought the tiny
terror.

It was just enough of a distraction for him not to
see the papaya launched straight for his head, which
caught him full on. Jeremy staggered badly and nearly fell
over, but managed to grab the wall and sink only a bit.

"Are you fuzzy kidding me?" He slurred.

Matilda levitated an entire bowl of Brussels
sprouts and individually shot each one at Jeremy, pegging
him all over his body, but aimed more than a few at his
crotch. She then threw an apple above his head and

exploded it into apple sauce so he couldn't avoid getting completely covered in it.

"Okay! Okay! I give up!" Jeremy yelled. "I'm Sorry!"

"Oh ya sorry are ya?" Matilda said smugly, "Guess where this asparagus is going?"

Jeremy immediately grabbed his butt with both hands. Matilda, dropped the greens and rapidly pegged him in the face with a rotten tomato.

"You called my mum to tattle on me ya bastard?" She roared, then send a cucumber rocket straight for his throat, but Jeremy fell over before it could make contact.

"I wasn't calling her, she was calling me, you left the pickled cats eyes in her car!" Jeremy mumbled.

"Oh…" Matilda said, calming down, "I were look'n for them."

The Rough Road

Prompts: Shanghai
Disclaimer: modern day redneck cowboys, southern accents

Old Wilber and young Tim-Tim ambled down the road in their makeshift wagon. It used to be a Ford F-250 pickup truck, but it had given up the horse power engine several years back in favor of some rather stout bulls.

"Hey Wilber...wutz that?" Tim-Tim asked and pointed down the road.

As they crept forward a black-haired woman on the largest jackass they'd ever seen was headed straight for them. She rode up on them like a spring storm and swiftly pulled a six-shooter out with practiced ease.

"Hold it boys!" She smiled with a raised eyebrow. Her red, pink and black plaid shirt was tight enough to give Tim-Tim zipper burn and Wilber a heart attack.

"Wuts hap'nen Tim-Tim?" Wilber scrunched up his bushy eyebrows.

"I recken we get'n shanghai'd Wilber," Tim-Tim replied, a bit surprised and turned-on at the same time.

"Thas right boys. Now gimme them goodies." The plaid hottie motioned with her gun.

Wilber looked at Tim-Tim and shrugged his shoulders.

"I guess ye better give it to'er," Wilber said.

Tim-Tim reached into the back of the pick-up wagon and grabbed a damp burlap sack, which he handed to the woman. She snatched it greedily and then opened the bag up to look inside.

"Xactly who is you boys deliver'n this bag of cat heads too?" She asked wide-eyed.

75

"Deliver'n?" Wilber asked a bit confused, "we pick'n up."

Creeping In

Prompts: Betrayed by one little sound, dropping the keys
at critical moment, screaming even though no one can
hear you

The Tarantula King slowly pushed open the door to
his office and peered inside. It was dark. It shouldn't have
been. He'd left a light on to prevent banging one of several
knees on the various coffee tables and end tables between
the door and his desk. He breathed in and out slowly.
Checking his pockets, he'd forgotten his cellphone in the
hearse and he didn't carry a flashlight. A few steps into the
room were safe, so he stood there waiting for his eight
eyes to adjust.

The floor board to his left creaked and startled
him, he involuntary dropped his keys. A red glow slowly
beamed from the corner as the Black Widow revealed
herself. She pounced on him without delay and rode him
straight to the floor.

"So, it was you who..." The Tarantula King realized,
swallowing hard.

"Indeed my king, it was yes-yes," She seethed.

"Am I supposed to be surprised?" He replied.

"You're about to be very... pleased." The Black
Widow smiled as she began to unbutton his tuxedo shirt.

77

The House

Prompt: Your biggest fear (but can't been named outright)

Beatrix opened her front door and entered tentatively, as if uncertain it was even her house. Her head peeked around the corner like a rabbit checking for danger from its burrow. She closed the door and moved into the living room with trepidation. It was empty.

She moved into the adjoining dining room attached to the kitchen. A few cat toys were scattered around the floor, but no feline to be seen. The space seemed to urge her forward at an elevated pace, she surged onward like a silent guided missile, seeking out its target. After a complete circuit of the first floor, Beatrix headed upstairs.

The first small bedroom was vacant of anything living. She gripped the doorjamb hard enough to rip the molding off, but let go just as she felt it move the tiniest bit. The bathroom door was open, displaying a clinical absence of dirt, hair or even germs. Beatrix, breathed in with little sips, the reality setting in on her. There were only two more rooms.

She opened the door to the sewing room and found the same result, an empty room. Finally entering her bedroom, she confirmed her greatest fear. Beatrix broke down crying, she crumpled to the floor and clutched a scarf which was hanging off her dresser. The memory of her husband and daughter flooded Beatrix's vision until she passed out from the grief.

Disclaimer: The fear was of being alone.

The Run In

Prompts: Write two scary lines/ sentences.

Vince was running late for the train and careened straight into a large man in a trench coat with an oversized suitcase. They rebounded off one another, both falling to the ground, the strangers suit case flew open, and spilled fresh human body parts across the sidewalk.

Another First

Prompts: A short trip.

Titus stepped out of his ship and looked around. The landscape was filled with purple grass, yellow trees and florescent pink bird-like creatures flitting about the purple sky. Checking his life suit diagnostics, it confirmed the presence of oxygen and nitrogen, breathable air. Titus removed his jump-helmet and took a tentative breath in through his nose. The entire planet smelled of candy corn, the kind you can only find during Halloween back on Earth.

Titus took a few steps forward and tripped, but caught himself before falling over. Luckily the suit was designed to improve his balance for just such a thing. Knelling down, he brushed away the purple grass to reveal a white object protruding from the soil. He took out a spade and began to dig around the object, excavating it. In just a few minutes, he'd freed it from the ground and rolled it around until it settled above ground. He stood up and stared at it. Before him was a human-like skull, with bone horns like a devil and an evil grin. The bizarre features aside, the skull was over three feet across.

Titus touched his onboard communication module to connect with the main ship.

"This is Titus, to USS Kelvin," He spoke.

"Go for Kelvin," a crystal-clear voice responded.

"You are not going to believe...." Titus stopped speaking as the skull began to float off the ground and parts of a body began to fall out of the skull, forming a complete corpse, which then grew its flesh like an unfolding gruesome flower.

"Yoooouuu…..are not welcome here!" The twenty-foot giant boomed in a voice like living death.

Too Late for That

Prompts: John Steinbeck quote "Don't make me mean"
Disclaimer: Herkimer has a heavy bass voice, Laslow's
voice is very nasally

Herkimer towered over Laslow, a low growl emanating from him.

"Don't look at me like that, it's your fault!" Laslow insisted, looking up at the giant, over two heads taller than him.

"My fault? You ran into me...little pipsqueak!" Herkimer boomed.

"Yeah, because you're taking up the whole isle! How's anyone supposed to get by you?" Laslow spelled out.

"You spilled your ale on me!" Herkimer's voice rose and he pointed at his tunic, with a finger the size of a summer sausage.

"You really trying to blame that on me?" Laslow squeaked and smacked the wet spot.

"Don't make me mean...or you'll become a stain on the floor." Herkimer said through gritted teeth.

"Hey, we'll have none of that in here you two," the bar maid spoke up, "you take that out yonder!"

"Yeah, see," Laslow said sarcastically, "she knows it's your fault!" He smacked the wet spot again.

Herkimer turned bright red and grabbed Laslow's entire body in one massive paw, picked him up so they were eye to eye.

"You're right, it's my fault....but I don't like you." Herkimer grinned.

He shoved Laslow's head straight up into the ceiling, then let go. The tiny body ran wildly in the air, arms and legs not making contact with anything.

"Yer gonna have ta pay for dat!" The barmaid yelled.

"Worth every schilling...gimmie another ale wench," Herkimer smiled with satisfaction.

Look at This

Prompts: Viewpoint of God, viewing a man who is cursing him

Archangel Michael ran through heaven as quickly as he could, carrying an iCloud Pad in both hands. He half flew over a section, then landed at the pearly gates and cleared his throat.

"Lord, are you...available?" Michael carefully annunciated, knowing how much sloppy diction annoyed God.

"Yes Michael, enter." God's voice boomed.

Archangel Michael swiftly entered the Lords chambers and stopped in front of a massive desk, which looked like a planet's topography laid out flat. The Lord looked up, and nodded his head.

"You really need to see this," Michael extended the iCloud Pad.
The lord snapped his fingers and the iCloud expanded onto the entire floor. The two looked down at a man in a small apartment who was actively cursing the Lord directly, for not fixing his life problems, which were clearly his own doing. For the grand finale, the man fake cried about it, not even able to generate real tears.

The Lord started to laugh and Archangel Michael got the giggles.

"This is the best!" The Lord slapped his knee, "I never get tired of these people who destroy their own lives, then get mad at me when I don't fix it! The nerve! I'm so glad I gave them nerve...always good for a laugh!"

"Yes, as soon as I saw him I got here as quick as I could," Michael chuckled.

"Put that up on Heaven-Tube, the other angels with get a kick out of that." God nodded.

"Posted. Oh wow, 3 trillion likes already!" Michael smiled. "What's that you're working on?"

"Oh...I've been noodling around with Sirius B...I think I'm going to reset the planet...instead of cat people...this time I'm going to try a race of conscious fruit beings..." God mused.

"I can't wait to see that!" Michael smiled, "Do they grow on trees?"

Last Act

Prompts: Things you spend time on: the yard, designing,
guitar, (the gym) dead lifts, reflecting, others, hair
Inspired quote: "All we have to decide is what to do with
the time given us." - J. R. Tolken
Disclaimer: Roland is an old man with a raspy voice

Roland picked up the guitar blueprint he'd been
designing and sighed deeply. It wasn't good enough.
Hearing a soft meow, he looked down and saw Raffles, his
severely overweight cat, looking up at him and rubbing
against his leg.

"I know, I know." Roland glumly acquiesced.

He leaned over and attempted to carefully pick up
his companion, but it was more like dead lifting a small
corpse.

"Why don't you work out at the gym Raffles?" He
asked, attempting a small bit of humor.

Raffles meowed again and settled into Roland's lap
for a nap, purring gently.

Roland was suddenly blinded by sunlight coming
through the window, the sun was just starting to set.
Turning the other way, he caught himself in the mirror.
His image appeared to be reflecting on something rather
important, much more so than he could fathom. Roland
ran his fingers through his once thick hair, now more of a
scraggly bird's nest. He looked back out the window, his
yard was overgrown with wild flowers, Gloria's final gift to
him. All he'd wanted to do was make a guitar worthy of
the sounds she used to play...but also, that seemed to
complement her beauty.

Raffles popped up, ears perky and meowed loudly.

"Yes Raffles, I suppose... all we have to decide is what to do with the time given us....you choose to eat too much...I choose this endless quest for a Love I can no longer see....but at least we're here together my furry friend."

With that, Raffles sneezed heavily in response, jumped down and ran away.

"Hey! I didn't mean it like that!" Roland cried out, then sighed and stared at his table of blueprints before standing up and walking to the window, closing his eyes and drinking in the sunlight on his skin, doing his best to feel her next to him.

Ancient Feeling

Prompts: Things that are easy to explain - Happiness, urgency, tying your shoelaces, falling, politics, recipe, how to cross the street, using a light switch, two times table, sweat, blinking

Sub-prompt: Quote can be used as inspiration: "The longer I live the more uninformed I feel, only the young have an explanation for everything."

The thought of a Love triangle, has a stigma about it. Most people will never be in one, so they really won't ever know the true feeling behind it. The older generations feel left behind with all the information out in the open, while the youth is taking to it like a fish to water, which isn't always a good thing. Kleo sat opposite two others, wondering these thoughts...realizing that she was on the older end of this internal dialog by a least a few thousand years. Charlie and Ursula had no idea, but they thought they did.

"Who wants to start?" Kleo asked.

Both of them looked uncomfortable.

"I can pick.... it's just like flipping a light switch for me..." Kleo broke the tension.

"I don't like feeling like I did something wrong, when I didn't!" Ursula stammered out.

"Well, it's not like you didn't know!" Charlie yelled.

"Hey now, there was no commitment between us....if anyone should feel bad it should be Kleo! She was messing with both of us!" Ursula yelled back.

"I've been dealing with this since before you two could tie your shoelaces...or cross the street for that matter." Kleo said calmly.

"Oh, let's not forget the whole part where she's a fucking vampire!" Ursula spat out.

"Hey, there's no need to be nasty, she's not taking advantage of us," Charlie retorted.

Ursula blinked several times, trying to read Charlie.

"You don't know do you...she's a vampire....like a drinking blood, live forever vampire." Ursula said.

Charlie broke out into a fit of laughter then looked at Kleo who had a slight smirk on her face. This stopped him laughing and a bead of sweat broke out on his forehead, racing down his left cheek.

"Do either of you even understand what constitutes real happiness?" Cleo casually asked.

"I know what falling in Love is." Charlie stated.

"You might as well be asking him about politics or the two times table...he can't comprehend what's happening! Look at him!" Ursula displayed both her hands directed at Charlies face.

"Listen, I enjoy both of you...if that's not enough for you two, you are free to leave. I'll find someone else to play with over the next century." Kleo smiled.

"What are you talking about?" Charlie was nervous, a sense of urgency in his voice.

"This..." Ursula pointed her finger and swirled it around to include the three of them, "is a recipe for an outcome I don't want to be involved in."

"Really? The outcome could be eternal life..." Kleo smiled.

All Day Drive

Prompts: Fictionalize something that happened during
the week
disclaimer: This is based on an all-day multi-state drive.

Jason stared out the windshield at the obscure landscape. Could he even call this a road? It was more like a warn path...well, a heavily trafficked route... it's not like there was a lot of other vehicles to contend with...but still.

"Are we almost there?" Ava asked.

"Does it look like we are?" Jason asked back.

"It might... if you told me where we're going. You've been driving for hours. You know I can drive too." Ava reminded him.

"Yes, I know that Ava, but then I might fall asleep and that thought makes me uncomfortable," Jason confessed.

"My driving makes you nervous?" Ava needled him.

"That's not the word I used..." He minced.

"Is it our age difference?" Ava reasoned.

"Why would you ask that?" Jason scrunched up his face thinking about it.

"Well...you are a LOT older than I am," Ava pointed out.

"Hey, I'm not that old in human years, thirty-three is still young!" Jason defended himself. "Aren't you supposed to put me at case while driving? You're advertised to be the most advanced model."

"Yes, I am on both accounts. Which is exactly why I asked those questions. I was manufactured exactly five hundred and one days ago." Ava pointed out.

"Yes, you're the most top of the line anti-gravity vehicle in this sector of the solar system, but no one told me you'd be so feisty!" Jason chuckled.

93

"I'm not feisty," Ava pouted. "Are we almost there?"

Hip Devil

Prompts: Something You think you shouldn't do that you do anyway: buy things for yourself, Smoke cigarettes, drink whiskey, vape, speak your mind
disclaimer: Start writing as if in the middle of the story

The explosion took them both by surprise, more Carl than the Devil, which made him wonder if the lord of the underground was behind it.

"I told you I was coming back didn't I, Carl?" The Devil eyed him and licked his lips with a forked tongue, then simultaneously smoked a cigarette, while vaping and puffing on a cigar.

"You're really trying to get some attention, aren't you?" Carl motioned.

"Oh? Does my smoking bother you Carl? Perhaps I should become a spend-a-holic like you and buy myself as many possessions as possible until I have to sell my soul to....oh wait, I can't do that," The Devil chuckled and grinned slyly.

"I do my best okay?" Carl professed.

"Your best?" The Devil stared, then swallowed all three smoking implements, washing them down with an entire bottle of Jack Daniels whiskey.

"I feel like you aren't even listening to me," Carl grimaced.

"No-no, speak your mind Carl, say what ya gotta say," the Devil urged him.

"You're not gonna like it," Carl confessed, "but I gave you a counterfeit soul."

"What? Where did you get a fake soul?" The Devil stared, wide awake.

"I 3D printed one." Carl smiled.

95

The Lambo Lambada

Prompts: Pick a bucket list item and write about it
disclaimer: Everything goes sideways in the story

It felt like a dream...the fact I was standing in front
of a 1974 Lamborghini Countach LP400s quatrovalve in
mint condition and repainted in metallic cobalt blue, was
so unbelievable....the odds were staggering. I swayed a bit
and had to grab a hold of the driver side door.

"I can tell you like it," Mustafar said.

"I don't have the words," I said, after trying to find
them. "I've always wanted to drive this exact car."

"Well my friend, let's take a drive." Mustafar
handed me the keys.

We both got in and I started the engine, which purred like
a dragon, ready to breath fire.

"Before we start, I must ask one thing of you,"
Mustafar looked me in the eye, "drive this vehicle as if it
was your car."

I smiled, slammed it into first gear and we were
thrust into our seats so hard I could feel my teeth trying to
escape my mouth. The first turn came up and the
Lamborghini cornered like it was glued to the road, no
slippage or loss of power. We hit a straightaway and I
opened it up to Mach 5, shifting through   all the gears
like I was breathing them out. Then it felt like we were
flying, like we'd left the ground. It was a foreign sensation.
I then felt a drop and I let this blue land born spacecraft
decelerate until we came to a crisp stop.

"How do you feel?" Mustafar asked me.

"I feel....like it's part of my soul." I smiled.

"Good." Mustafar smiled, "because I'm giving you
this car to keep."

Never Trick a Sorceress

Prompts: Something you can believe in without Seeing: magic, pixies, fate, humanity, God, wind, my ancestors, faith

Lucas had been falling for what felt like several minutes, unable to see anything in front of him. The ground suddenly appeared mere inches from his face, which was promptly smashed, along with the rest of him. He couldn't feel a single part of his body that wasn't in pain, but he had faith that something, at least one thing...wasn't broken. A set of finely booted feet approached his head.

"I'm....sorry," Lucas managed with great difficulty.

"You dare speak to me?" Lyla intoned.

She snapped her fingers and pixies surrounded Lucas, then grabbed him all over and stood his body upright so it faced the divinely gorgeous sorceress.

"One more time peasant? I don't think I heard you," Lyla spoke with slight irritation.

"I didn't...I wasn't trying too..." Lucas mumbled.

Lyla waved her hand sharply, a gust of wind forcibly hit Lucas and knocked him free of the pixies grasp. He landed on his back with a loud crack.

"Oh...mylanta..." Lucas moaned.

"Are you an old woman?" Lyla stared at him in disbelief.

"God save me," he whined.

"God? God's not coming for you! Neither are your ancestors, the villagers down the hill or the herd of jackalopes in that tiny cave...no one is going to help you!" Lyla yelled.

"If it is my fate to die here....you can go fuck yourself you wretched witch," Lucas spat out, then coughed up some blood.

"You deceive me...try to steal MY MAGIC and I'm in the wrong? Do I have that correct?" Lyla asked in disbelief.

"For that you dropped me from the edge of the sky...but kept me alive just so I could feel the pain...you are the worst...creature..." Lucas breathed with difficulty.

"You will be no loss to humanity..." Lyla said snidely.

Lucas burst into flames, viciously burning into a heap of blackened earth.

"Fire..." Lyla pondered, "I didn't put any fire in the spell...."

The blacked ashes shifted and moved, until Lucas stood up, naked but uninjured.

"Cute....you're a phoenix...you should have led with that lover boy," Lyla eyed him and smiled.

Now You Tell Me

Prompts: Moderation
Disclaimer: Heavy Germanic Accents

Herman was latched onto some tiny village woman's neck, drinking her dry. Sally, her name was...blood that had hints of strawberries in it. Phyllis threw open the barn doors and stood silhouetted in the moonlight.

"Herman! Vhat is wrong vith you!" Phyllis chastised him.

He immediately dropped Sally's body to the floor.

"Vhat? Vhat did I do?" Herman asked without a clue.

"Don't you give me zhat act! I vake you from four decades slumber and zhis is how you behave?" Phyllis demanded.

"Vhat...I vas thirsty?" Herman struggled his shoulders.

Phyllis flipped on the single lightbulb in the barn to reveal a pile of bodies...possibly twenty or more.

"Thirsty...no...you are a pig! Look at zhis pile of bodies! Zhere is such a ting as moderation you greedy selfish lout." She informed him with disappointment, slowly shaking her head.

"Vell...ah...did you vant von?" Herman asked with raised sharp eyebrows.

"Oh, how thoughtful of you to tink of your sister...yes I would like, OH WAIT YOU ATE EVERYONE!" Phyllis yelled.

"I am vampire, vhat you vant from me?" Herman threw up his arms in frustration.

"You could have behaved like a normal man, gotten a six-pack to share vith me...like...a full SUV...and ve could

101

have taken in a nice movie vhile ve ate!" Phyllis stared at him plainly.

"Oh no...did you feed ze verevolf?" Herman asked.

"Scheisse...mine forgot," Phyllis grimaced.

Oh, That's just Bob

Prompts: The Hanged Mans resolutions

Toby and Henry stood about forty feet away from the tree, just staring. There was a man hanging upside-down in the tree.

"Well? Do you know him or not?" Toby pressed insistently.

"I...um..." Henry squinted his eyes, "I'm pretty sure that's Bob."

The two small boys both squinted their eyes.

"Wait, which Bob? The barber? The butcher? The baker?" Toby pondered.

"I wrecken I'm not fer sure...it just now occurred to me...all three of them Bobs look alike," Henry confessed.

"You think he needs help?" Toby wondered.

"Naw, he don't need nuthin...he's smile'n," Henry nodded his head.

"I'm gonna go talk to 'em." Toby decided.

"Are you crazy? You never talk to a old fart hanging upside down from a tree, smilin' like a duck!" Henry exclaimed.

This gave Toby pause for just a moment.

"You jus said that like it was a thing...but you made it up, didn't cha?" Toby stared at Henry.

"Fine, don't believe me, go on." Henry said, and crossed his arms.

Toby paused for a second, then walked swiftly over to the tree and looked up at Bob, which ever one he was, and thought about what to say...his eyes were closed, but he was indeed smiling, like he was dreaming about something funny.

"Hey mister!" Toby called out.

The man opened his eyes, then suddenly fell out of the tree, right in front of Toby.

"You one of them Bobs?" Toby insisted.

"How many of me do you see kid?" The man asked uneasily.

"Just one...wait, are there more Bob's in the tree?" Toby asked looking up at the branches, "you is Bob right?"

"Yeah, I'm Bob..." Bob affirmed.

"Yeah, but which Bob?" Toby asked.

"Oh, I'm Bob the Banker." He answered, again smiling with his eyes closed.

Too Much Gumshoe

Prompts: Something that makes you lose your cool: A mess that you didn't make, a hot bath, having to repeat myself, lies, being asked to wait five more minutes, miscommunication, lack of thoughtfulness
Disclaimer: Set in the 1930's

Harry shuffled down the dark street, stepped off the curb to cross the road and went ankle deep into a puddle.

"Ah crap." He fussed and shook out his wet foot. "One more suit ruined," he mumbled and tightened up his trench coat, then adjusted his Stetson at the brim.

Harry looked up at the hotel's bright neon sign, sighed and headed inside. A woman in her mid-thirties was waiting for him. She was a bit disheveled.

"You Dolores?" Harry nodded.

"Yeah, that's right. You the gumshoe?" Dolores looked him up and down.

"Private Detective, thanks." Harry corrected her.

"Well Mr. Privates, ya look like a hot bath would fix a lotta things for ya," Dolores said with raised eyebrows as she wrinkled her nose.

"You gonna waste my time all night?" Harry dead eyed her.

She stared back at him and then picked up a phone, hit a few buttons and waited.

"Yeah, he's here....uhuh....ya, okay." Dolores said and hung up the phone. "Can ya wait five minutes?"

"Are you serious lady? What's a dead guy care about when I walk in to investigate?" Harry was irritated.

"I don't like repeat'n myself mista, ya gotta wait five minutes," Dolores eyeballed him hard.

"Maybe there was a miscommunication here," Harry motioned with his hands between the two of them, "I'm here to help you out, so the cops ain't involved. Now, if you'd like that to happen, time is of the essence sweet cheeks." Harry smiled at the last bit, trying to appear friendly.

"Oh, you're one of them," She spat out.

"There's only one of me, that's right." Harry agreed.

"Nah, that ain't what I meant. You think yor all suave, but ya ain't got an ounce of thoughtfulness in ya." Dolores said and crossed her arms.

"I think plenty," Harry smiled, "I just don't think much'a you."

A large man pounded down the stairs, he was pushing three hundred pounds, about six foot five, Cuban and mean looking.

"You the boss?" Harry asked.

"I'm the cleaning lady," the man said gruffly.

"What is the problem exactly?" Harry asked.

"The problem is, the dead guy melted a hole from the room on the fourth floor to the room underneath on the third floor." The large man said straight-faced with a bass laden tone.

"I didn't make dis mess, but I'm gonna clean it up." Harry shook his head and headed up the stairs.

Impure Escape
Prompts: Seeing Things More Clearly

Jerry was running as hard as he could, his breathing was out of control, vision blurring, trees flying by at breakneck speed. Without warning, he slipped on a patch of bear shit and fell off the ridge, tumbling down into the marsh. He splashed about wildly, trying to get his bearings, but it was too late. The hairy beast that was hunting him had jumped in the muddy water on top of him.

Jerry thrashed and fought back, but the creature was too strong. Its massive paws latched on to him and drug him from the marsh water onto land. At some point his body went limp. The beast released him to the ground and sniffed him about the head and torso. Despite being wet, Jerry broke out in fever sweats. His body was shaking uncontrollable.

"No! NO! Don't eat me!" Jerry cried out.

The creature huffed, a bit of a laugh if you could call it that. It then bit him gently on the arm. Jerry could feel the venom coursing through his veins. It burned like lava, trying to melt him from the inside. Once he felt like the end was near and he was about to die, the heat subsided. Jerry opened his tightly squeezed eyelids to see the beast still lingering over him. His blurred vision began to shift and the hairy monster gradually altered its shape. Jerry shook his head and Malinda's face came into view. She was smiling down at him.

"Can you hear me now Jerry?" Malinda asked softly.

"What....what happened? You...where's the monster?" Jerry asked, looking around.

"It's back inside you my Love." Malinda stroked his head, "Let's go home."

Just Do It

Prompts: Something to be Proud of - flow, my cooking, family, getting out of bed in the morning, good amount of exercise, kindness, skills, unapologetic degeneracy, yourself.

Mildred felt the sunlight hitting her left eye...it was annoying. She pulled the covers up over her head, but the thin material barely did a thing to help. She sighed inwardly and threw the covers to the side, then hopped out of bed. "Get up at the crack of dawn" her master always told her. She often thought of responding with, "I don't want to see Dawns butt crack!" However, she didn't feel like reciting sanitation spells all day.

Her bare toes touched the floor and she immediately hopped into her slippers to avoid the chill. You'd think living in a tree would be warmer, but it wasn't. She missed living with her family, it had been so long since she'd had a warm bundle of bodies to snuggle against.

Mildred immediately went right into her morning exercise routine, her master had driven it into her so hard, if she even thought of doing something else first, it brought on a wave of shame. Kindness was not one of her masters' virtues. He was a hard muskrat to please. He was also an unapologetic degenerate, constantly staring at her body like it was his own personal playground. Thank goodness there were others in the class to distract him. Plus, he wasn't that into squirrels. He just happened to be the only certified training wizard in the forest, or she'd have gone somewhere else. Mildred had gotten into her flow, moving her body and the energy around her. She began casting spells as she did her sit ups to start the stove cooking her breakfast.

109

Mildred was proud of herself for graduating top of her class and winning the right to have her own maple tree house. It was hard work, but she was now the sorceress of an entire forest quadrant.

A presence caught her attention, she stopped moving to focus on it. A pulse was coming from the western window. Mildred grabbed her wand and quickly moved to the window, just as a large yellow scaly claw broke into her home, grabbed her bodily and ripped her outside the tree, simultaneously she cast a lightning spell against her attacker. The two began to fall, ground rapidly approaching, Mildred caught a glimpse of what had grabbed her, eyes wide at the monster which wasn't supposed to exist.

Just Do It - Part 2

Prompts: Playing Defense

Mildred was able to cast a growth spurt spell as she fell, striking a small fern below her. It sprang up like an explosion, just large enough to cushion her hundred-foot fall. She careened off to the right and landed on all fours, then quickly moved backward as the stunned creature hit the forest floor, just barely missing her. Mildred jumped onto a tree and ran up a bit before looking back at the beast. She'd only read about them in books, over ten feet tall, covered in thickly armored scales with spikes protruding from jointed limbs, there was no doubt....it was a Rootscag.

Long ago these creatures used to devour entire forests. Trees and inhabitants alike. One of its three eyes opened and stared right at her. Its tail swung hard, aimed right for her position. She jumped swiftly, and latched onto a nearby tree.

"You are trespassing on protected grounds!" Mildred yelled.

"You can't even protect your own tree! You pathetic snack!" The Rootscag growled to her surprise.

Mildred cast a fireball spell at the beast, who curled up in defense, taking the brunt of the attack on its back. The flames washed off the scales and dispersed, showing no sign of affecting it in the slightest.

"That tickled!" The Rootscag hissed with a forked tongue. He then spat out a stream of viscous venom, which caught Mildred in her left leg and tail, causing her to fall to the ground.

The Rootscag stood up at full height, towering over her. Mildred couldn't move, the venom entering her

111

system, her eyes watery and burning. Just as the massive mouth full of teeth lunged for her, Mildred cast a turtle shell shield. Instantly she was encased in the protective spell, her best defensive weapon. The Rootscag swallowed her whole.

"Great, I'm never going to hear the end of this from Master Krick…'How could you let yourself be swallowed?'" Mildred sighed inwardly and rolled her eyes.

Just Do It - Part 3
Prompts: Pure Joy

Mildred watched her progression down the Rootscags long distended throat and landed in its rather sizable stomach.

"This is almost half the size of my house!" Mildred mused, then doubled over in pain. The venom was wreaking havoc on her tiny squirrel body. She tried to figure out a way to deal with the poison in her system, just as the stomach opened some valve, dumping a large amount of yellow acid into it. Suddenly she was submerged and wondering how long her spell would hold. The body was jarred without warning. To the left, then to the front, it felt as though the Rootscag was running or jumping around. She felt the ground slam upward. All at once, there was light pouring into the stomach, the acid was draining, she slid out of the Rootscags body to the smiling face of Brenda.

"I knew you'd been swallowed!" Brenda smiled and shook her massively furry head.

Mildred dropped the turtle shell spell and looked up painfully.

"Brenda, how did you know?" Mildred asked, confused how the large magic infused grizzly bear had come to her rescue.

"Oh, I saw you falling with that big yellow beastie and I came running! When I got here and your smell was all over that thing, I just knew it! So, ya know...kill'em with kindness! I hugged it, until it popped! Then I dug you out! That made me so happy!" Brenda smiled widely.

"Brenda, you're the bestest bear I know," Mildred smiled weakly.

Relaxing Weekend

Prompts: Things that go together (like peanut butter and jelly): ham and burgers, marshmallows and campfire, sex and cigarettes, women and screaming, therapy and chocolate, mashed potatoes and gravy, puddles and jumping, rocks and scissors.

Charles stared at the grill and sighed inwardly. Sarah insisted he cook burgers as well as ham steak. Why? It made no sense to him, but rather than upset her, he just did it. Charles was overly sensitive and a woman screaming at him on the weekend when he's supposed to be decompressing from the stress of the week, would have just sent him over the edge. Even thinking these thoughts was getting him worked up. His father's words were ringing in his head, "Don't be such a wussy Chucky!" He'd hated that stupid moniker as well...it reminded him of that killer doll movie. Now his breathing was elevated and he had to grab onto a patio chair for support.

"Did you remember to get the chocolate, marshmallows and graham crackers for the s'mores tonight? I want to make them like we do over a campfire," Sarah called out from the sliding door of the house.

Charles glanced over at her and nodded until she disappeared. He pushed off of the chair and went back to the grill. It was time to turn all the meats over. A noise caught his attention, something was going on in the neighbor's yard. They had small children who were almost always unsupervised. Charles closed the grill and went to the fence to peak over and see what they were doing. The scene was like a safety poster come to life.

Little Sammy was jumping up and down in a large puddle, apparently trying to remove all the water with his

115

feet. Katie was running around the yard with a rock, being chase by her younger brother Bobby with a set of those ridiculous plastic scissors that don't cut anything, why they give them to give kids was a mystery.

Smelling smoke, Charles turned to see the grill was smoking way more than it should be. He ran over, opened the top and quickly shifted all the burgers and ham steaks around so they didn't burn.

"Come on Charles, you can do better. No way she's gonna have sex tonight if all the food is burnt to a crisp!" Charles chided himself.

Sarah walked out of the house and lit a cigarette, put her hand on her hip and stared at him. The look she gave him was making him nervous. She walked over to him and plopped down on one of patio chairs, smoking angrily.

"What's wrong?" Charles asked, overly concerned.

"I burned the gravy and the potatoes are all chunky..." Sarah pouted. "I told you I can't cook!"

"Well, you aren't going to get any better if you don't try," Charlie reminded her.

"I don't need you to mansplain cooking to me!" Sarah answered, dripping with sarcasm.

"I didn't mean it like that Sarah! You-I'm just trying to....." Charlie cut himself off, breathing heavily.

"Oh great, the breathing again. Do you need to go to therapy now? You little weasel? Grow a pair of balls already! I'm so sick and tired of all your bullshit! You can't do anything without having a total mental breakdown! Be a man!" Sarah yelled.

Charles stared at her, eyes burning red, his breathing had stopped. He slowly turned around, picked up a pair of tongs, grabbed the largest ham steak, then spun around and slapped Sarah right in the face with it so hard she fell out of the chair.

"Here's your dinner honey! Enjoy your fucking s'mores!" Charles yelled, dropped the tongs on the ground and stormed off into the house, slamming the door so hard the screen flew off the track and scared his obese cat Oscar.

The Dripping Pony
Prompts: Differing Perspectives

Lucas tightened up his heavy armored trench coat against the night's chill. He took deep strides as he walked up to the tavern, grasped its centuries old blacksmithed wrought iron door handle and retched open the solid oak entrance. The Dripping Pony was not only a stupid name for a pub, but a total hole in the ground.

Lucas looked around, then spotted Vanessa. He walked casually over to her booth and sat down opposite her. She acknowledged him with a nod. He reached out with his hand and touched hers. Connected, now they could speak mentally without being overheard.

"How long have they been here?" Lucas asked.

"Well, I've been sitting here for nearly two hours. So at least that long." Vanessa relayed.

"So....tell me what you see." Lucas inquired.

He was asking about a man and a woman who were sitting at the bar together, drinking enough whiskey to kill a small village. Vanessa stared and picked out her words carefully.

"The man is definitely a vampire. I can't tell what the woman is...she feels...off. Possibly a witch? I've mostly been listening to them." Vanessa explained.

"And what have you learned?" Lucas asked.

"Nothing...they haven't said anything of use. I did hear them mention a few names, but I couldn't place them." Vanessa was frustrated.

"Did you not notice the three dark elves sitting across the room, staring at them?" Lucas asked.

Vanessa shifted her attention and immediately saw the three gritty looking men, dressed in heavy leather

119

coats, hugging a round table filled with several empty beer pitchers.

"They're going to cause a problem, aren't they?" Vanessa asked.

"They can be allies, but the woman….she's not a witch…she's a necromancer." Lucas relayed.

Vanessa snapped her head around to lock eyes with Lucas.

"What is the protocol for a necromancer?" Vanessa asked, obviously nervous about seeing her first death sorceress.

"Necromancers are very difficult," Lucas cut himself short and keyed in on the front door, "Oh shit."

He'd barely gotten the words out before the door opened and six rotting corpses staggered inside. Lucas activated both of his wrist mounted Damascus auto-gauntlets, which covered each fist with hard wired Atlantian magic infused metal weapons. "This is gonna get ugly…we're gonna have bystander bodies dropping."

"What do we do?" Vanessa asked, alarm in her voice.

Before he could answer the dark elves jumped into action, engaging all six ghouls. The pub erupted into chaos. Lucas looked back at the bar to find the vampire and necromancer had vanished.

"The necromancer pulled the ghouls in," Lucas grimaced. "We just got duped."

Bed Time

Prompts: A Sex scene, keyword 'Lollipop'

Brittany checked the mirror one last time, her long blonde hair was perfectly curled, makeup was flawless and all her leather straps were cinched tight. She winked at herself and exited the bathroom.

Kevin was sitting on the bed, like he was patiently waiting at a doctor's office. When Brittany entered the room, his jaw just dropped and his eyes disparately tried to escape his body and roll all over her tight curves.

Brittany sauntered over to Kevin and pushed him down on the bed, then began slowly taking off his clothes.

"You know what I want don't you?" She moaned.

"What...I...I...got it for you baby," Kevin stammered, his heart racing.

"Gimmie that lollipop daddy," she smiled, "I've been a good girl."

She pulled down his boxer briefs and there was his watermelon berry blast. She shoved it right into her mouth and his entire body shuddered. He had no idea how long she was licking before he opened his eyes and she was on top of him, riding slowly like she was on a fifty-cent grocery store rocket ship, taking him straight into out space.

An Uncomfortable Time

Prompts: Things that always sound good - massage, hot chocolate, strawberry twizzlers, skiing and snowboarding, motorcycles, puppy, fairytale ending, asking for feedback, candle light

Zahn felt uncomfortable. He didn't like doing this kind of stuff, he was a pretty straight forward man's man. He liked his motorcycle, snowboarding on the weekends and chill'n with his new Australian Cattle Dog puppy. Instead, he was naked, except for a towel, laying on a table in a room illuminated by candle light. This was his girlfriend's Christmas gift to him.

"Hi, I'm Chloe, I'll be your massage therapist today. Is there any area's you want me to focus on?" Cloe asked sweetly.

"Naw, I'm good." Zahn said, like he didn't care.

"I see here this massage was a gift from someone and they had some special requests." Chloe said as she read something on an iPad.

"My girlfriend. This is her deal." Zahn continued blankly.

"Okay, let's flip you onto your stomach so I can get started on your back." Chloe instructed.

Zahn flipped over and put his head in a strange looking add on to the table which he called the 'table donut'.

A timer went off and Chloe grabbed a mug from a warmer and poured hot melted chocolate all down Zahn's back.

"Whooaaaa! AAhhhhh!" Zahn cried out.

"Stay still!" Chloe commanded.

The chocolate quickly hardened all over his back and Zahn realized it was the kind used for dipping ice cream cones.

"These are strawberry per the instructions," Chloe informed him.

"What?" Zahn was totally confused.

Chloe had two fist-fulls of strawberry twizzlers and began to beat Zahn's back with them, like she was trying to clean all the dried chocolate flakes off his skin. Instead, it felt like some kind of weird torture.

"Aren't you supposed to give me one of those fairytale endings or something?" Zahn called out.

"This isn't that kind of massage," Chloe informed him. "However, when I need any feedback, I'll ask you."

The Trudging Truth
Prompts: A Path through the Snow

Jeremy staggered forward at a ridiculous pace, forging a path through the knee-high snow. Looking behind him, there was nothing, but he knew that was a lie. He was being followed. This snow was only making it easier for him to be found. Everywhere he went, he was creating a giant line for his stalker. The forest wasn't consistent, he'd just made it through a wide-open field, but this area was more tree laden. Rounding a bend, he encountered a new fresh path in the snow. It was large, wider than his. The cold was getting to him, he couldn't reason if this was good or bad.

Jeremy stared at the new path and thought it looked like whatever made it was headed to the East, so he decided to go West. It led him deeper into the forest and straight to a cave entrance. Curiosity got the better of him. Jeremey turned on his cellphone flashlight and entered the cave. It only went straight for about ten feet before turning a bend and he couldn't believe his eyes.

Before him was a small burning fire, and a woman about his age wrapping in a bearskin. She looked up at Jeremey and jumped. Quickly getting up, she ran to the wall and grabbed a spear, which caused her bearskin to fall, and reveal a loud set of pink and black checkered onesie pajamas.

"Karen?" Jeremy was shocked.

"This is bullshit Jeremy! What part of I fucked your brother wasn't clear?" Karen yelled.

"What are you talking about?" Jeremy was totally confused.

"Didn't you get my text?" She asked, lowering the spear.

125

Pick of the Litter

Prompts: One thing you hate about yourself - Anger, sleeping pattern, martyr complex, overextending myself, bad back, need for control, my voice, indecisiveness, height.

Jerry stared at his dog angrily sleeping and could only hear his ex-wife Samantha's voice on repeat in his head.

"You shouldn't get one of those shelter dogs! They're not right and we're gonna have to live with it for years!"

Apparently, only he would have to live with it, since she baled on him for some base player who had a cat.

Jerry had no idea dogs could sleep angry until he adopted Blinky. This dog's sleeping pattern was like a full-time job only he hated the job and kept trying to bite everything around him. Jerry at first thought it was the sound of his voice which was irritating the mixed breed mutt, but Blinky seemed perfectly fine when he was awake. Perhaps it was because he was height challenged. Blinky was about three feet long, but only four inches off the ground. It was mildly comical to see him run, but the mixed genealogy resulted in the poor fella having a bad back and Jerry had to take him to the pet chiropractor once a week. He didn't even know there *were* pet chiropractors before now.

Thinking back to the pound, he'd been a little indecisive about adopting Blinky. There was a more normal looking dog there, a collie, but something about Blinky was weirdly attractive, like when you see a terrible accident, but you can't look away. His ex-wife had this overwhelming need for control over everything and the fact that he picked the dog without her started the entire downward spiral in their relationship. At least he didn't have to worry about Blinky running off with a drummer...he just had to worry about losing a foot if he walked too close to his sleepy mutt.

The Mark
Prompt: Inside an arena

Boyin tracked his mark to a large outdoor arena, it was nearly midnight. It was not unlike the grand gladiator houses of old, but a much more modern version and severely under built. A shadow across the way caught his attention and he let loose a bio-shuriken. The spinning black star flew across the open space smoothly until the gyroscope popped out and it took a hard left, homing in on its target. Apparently, the mark saw it coming and changed directions again, but the star simply shifted with him and punched through his right leg, then slammed into a cinderblock wall.

Boyin drew a pistol and advanced. He could hear them struggling. Stepping into the inner entry, he spied a woman on the ground, trying to hold her leg together. The monofilament wire on the edges of the bio-shuriken had near amputated her leg. She was unarmed, but her head swung up to look at him and he was confronted with the demon eye. Boyin deployed his arm shield just in time to deflect the ray of demonic energy meant to kill him. Twisting to the side, flipping his trench coat up in a flowing display, he closed the gap between them rapidly and landed on top of her, pinning her shoulders to the ground with his knees. He grabbed her head, holding it steady with his left hand and snatched the demon eye straight out of her skull with his right hand.

"You're freed now," Boyin said.

"What's happening?" She cried.

"You were possessed...by this." Boyin held up the Demon eye, which looked like a blood-stained bone cylinder. It weirdly resembled a small laser pointer used to amuse a household pet.

"Why are you doing this to me?" She cried.

"I was hired to kill you," Boyin stated, "don't push it."

Today's the Day

Prompts: Peaceful actions or practices - breathing,
fishing, writing, caress, floating on your back in water,
painting, drawing

As Teaboo tightened his robe, he let loose a deep
breath out so his body would hold the robe tightly once he
inhaled. Smiling for this small victory, he looked out the
window at the brother monks who were already outside,
practicing various forms and meditations.

"Is today the day?" Noni asked.

"It feels like a good day, but who is to know such
things?" Teaboo answered.

"You still feel badly... don't you?" Noni asked.

"No...I don't...I... not anymore," Teaboo smiled.
"Time to get moving.

Teaboo exited his room and walked outside into
the courtyard. Walking through the various areas, he
observed a group of monks all painting a large Buddha. It
looked very colorful and joyous.

He continued walking further down towards the
forest and saw Brother Lee writing poetry in his journal.
Teaboo had always wanted to be a poet, but it wasn't his
strong suit. He detoured closer to steal a peak and saw
that today Brother Lee had also drawn lotus flowers in all
the blank spaces of the poem page.

Teaboo smiled and continued down to the lake.
Brother Cho was on his usual rock with a fishing pool,
attempting to catch a thousand-year-old dragon that lived
in the water.

"Any nibbles Brother Cho?" Teaboo inquired.

"Not yet," Brother Cho smiled in return.

Teaboo approached the water's edge and bent
down to caress the lake's surface gently.

131

"Today's the day," Noni cheered him on.

"Perhaps." Teaboo replied.

Teaboo waded out into the water and lay flat. He floated on his back and looked up at the sky, then closed his eyes. He focused all of his energy on being in the moment.

"You can do it," Noni encouraged him.

Teaboo smiled, felt his hands touch the surface of the water. He pushed off rapidly and sprung upward, standing on the water's surface, holding his balance.

"Brother Teaboo!" Brother Cho called out in amazement.

The distraction disrupted Teaboo's chi and he immediately fell back into the water.

"So close," Noni observed.

"Perhaps tomorrow," Teaboo smiled at the spirit of his sister who never left his side.

Teaboo's Sister

Prompts: An awareness of ghosts

Teaboo made his way out of the water to an eagerly waiting Brother Cho who dropped his fishing pole in awe. Teaboo smiled and wrung out his robe to return the lake back to its home.

"Your technique is amazing," Brother Cho smiled.

"It's a start," Teaboo grinned.

"He's almost ready," Noni agreed.

"Who was that?" Brother Cho asked and looked around.

"Did you hear Noni?" Teaboo asked with surprise.

"I heard a woman's voice," Brother Cho looked at Teaboo.

"So, you can hear me?" Noni asked.

"Yes! I hear you." Brother Cho looked next to Teaboo and focused.

"That's my twin sister Noni. She looks just like me, but shorter." Teaboo guided Brother Cho. "Can you see her?"

Brother Cho shook his head with a grimace.

"Focus on the sound of my voice and connect with me," Noni spoke softly.

Brother Cho honed all his senses on the poetic sound of Noni's whisper sweet voice. She continued to talk to him and little by little, blurbs of color began to peak through an invisible veil. Gradually a flower pattern floated in the air by itself, until rosie cheeks were above it. The more she spoke, the clearer she became, until Brother Cho saw a young woman, standing next to Teaboo, in a white kimono with a flower print moving across the front.

"It's nice to meet you Noni," Brother Cho bowed and smiled at her.

133

"And I you, Brother Cho," Noni smiled and bowed in return.

"Have you been with your brother all this time? Since his first year at the monastery?" Brother Cho inquired.

"I am always with him, we are inseparable," Noni answered. "By the way, someone else wants to say hello to you."

"Is there another ghost here?" Brother Cho asked with raised eyebrows.

Suddenly a large silver dragon burst forth from the lakes surface. It stared at the three of them, appearing to smile with a nod, before disappearing back into the depths of the water.

The Dark Truth
Prompts: Family Secrets

Teaboo, Noni and Brother Cho bathed in the afterglow of being blessed by the ancient silver dragon.

"I can't believe he's been there the entire time....watching me," Brother Cho mumbled.

"He really enjoys your dedication," Noni smiled at him.

"You speak to him?" Brother Cho asked.

"In a way, yes." Noni nodded.

"Wait...I feel as though we have missed...what happened to you? Why is Noni a ghost Teaboo?" Brother Cho focused back on the twins.

"It's a brutal story," Teaboo shied away.

"The truth about family can be brutal indeed," Brother Cho nodded.

"My father held a secret from us for many years," Noni averted her eyes, "a disgrace upon not only our family, but our village as well."

"I should tell the story, it's my job as the eldest sibling," Teaboo glanced sideways at his sister.

"Psshh, eldest by two minutes," Noni grinned, "but I agree, it's your responsibility."

"Please, go on." Brother Cho encouraged him.

"From the time we were small children, all the way up to the marrying age, our village suffered under the invisible threat of demon who randomly murdered people over the years. There were many rumors about the source of the demon and its true nature, but they were all much further from the truth, which lay within our own home." Teaboo took a breath in before continuing. "As it turned out, our father had been bitten by a weretiger shortly after we were born. Every full moon he would leave our home to

135

go roam the forest so he wouldn't kill us all. Anyone who happened to cross his path was ripped to pieces."

"So, what happened?" Brother Cho asked.

"There was an accident. Our father fell off the roof of our neighbors' house and broke his back. That night was the full moon and he couldn't escape into the forest. He turned right there in his bed and tore into our mother, killing her in seconds. Noni, ran into the room thinking an animal had somehow invaded from the forest. Father clawed her body nearly in half. I came running in with his Katana and sank it straight through his heart. He didn't die right away, but he did turn back. In his death throes he told us what happened. He begged me to atone for his deeds. That's why I joined the monastery."

"And I'm here to make sure he keeps his promise." Noni reminded him.

"These dark secrets are more common than you think," Brother Cho confessed.

Sneaking Peeks

Prompts: Something nostalgic - freshly baked chocolate chip cookies, Rainbow Brite, teenage mutant ninja turtles, Christmas tree lights on grandparents Christmas tree, grandma's green beans, sitting at the edge of the river

The sound of buzzing filled the room as Cindy stared at the lady laying down. She did her best to go unnoticed, creeping around quietly to get a look. She saw a plate of warm chocolate chip cookies that she wished she could grab. Near that was a ninja turtle with a long sword she'd never seen before. The adults shifted a bit and Cindy quickly ran out of the way so she wouldn't get yelled at. Peeking over a box, she saw an old classic looked Christmas tree, decorated with lights and a pair of old gray-haired faces on either side, maybe someone's grandparents.

"What are you doing Cindy?" Came Carl's gruff voice.

"Nothing daddy, I'm just look'n." She said in a small voice.

"You know who Rainbow Bright is?" Lilly asked her, to which Cindy shook her head. "Come take a look."

Cindy trotted close and saw the new tattoo her daddy was putting on this woman's arm. It was a little girl with rainbow colored hair and bright colorful clothing.

"She's pretty," Cindy smiled.

"Thank you!" Lilly smiled.

"Cindy, get your green bean snack and go sit by the river and eat or your mama will wax yer bottom." Carl warned her.

"Okay Daddy," Cindy smiled and grabbed her little backpack of stuff and headed out the back door.

The Custom Order

Prompts: A steam powered metal workshop set in the
future

Herman heard the loud hissing sounds long before
he opened the door. Of course, this wasn't his first trip to
Korman's Steam Machinery. Walking through the door,
there were massive lathes, iron workers, hydraulic presses
and other metal forming tools, all run off a centralized
steam power unit in the center of the workshop. Looking
around, doing his best to ignore the cacophony of sounds,
Herman spotted Flip over near one of the horizontal mills.
He made his way over carefully. Ever since to worldwide
breakdown of the Earth's magnetic field, electricity had
been impossible to use without causing massive
uncontrollable explosions. All the old methods of
production had resurfaced and been reinvented. Herman
tapped Flip on the shoulder after he finished making his
final pass on a block of aluminum. Flip smiled and nodded,
waving him to follow.

They walked down a ramp to a set of steel stairs
that zig-zagged through the plant. Finally, they arrived at
a room, which held what Herman had come to pick up.
Once inside, the noise level dropped enough for them to
speak.

"Well, what do you think?" Flip asked.

Herman picked up the metal block, turned it a few
times, looking at each unique textured side in leu of colors,
then nodded.

"Yup, it looks like a Rubik's cube! Thanks!" Herman
smiled and handed over a wade of cash.

Girls Night

Prompts: Things you used to do too much: philander,
think, overshare, night outs, text, talk, play games

Sasha stared at Kelly with disdain. She'd shown up
unannounced at her door and insisted on a girl's night out.
Now they were at one of those stupid dance clubs, with
thirsty looking guys wearing too much cologne and
dressing ten years younger than they should. The place
was probably infested with philanderers, whom she
wanted nothing to do with.

"This was such a good idea!" Kelly yelled over the
loud music.
Sasha gave a fake, rather catty smile in response and
sipped her white wine.

"Don't you think this club is awesome?" Kelly
giggled.

"Oh, it's totally the tits!" Sasha replied
sarcastically.

"You're so funny!" Kelly laughed and then got
distracted by a hot guy and ignored her.

As if a neon sign had just turned on pointing her
out, a beard toting, belly boasting, male of the species
made a bee line right for her. Sasha rolled her eyes and
braced herself for the stupid.

"Hey! I'm Jack, what's your name?" Jack smiled
and swayed to the music.

"Sasha," she replied.

"Not one to overshare! It's cool, I get it. This place
it a total meat market." Jack nodded.

"I'm not into playing games," Sasha announced.

"Hey it's cool, we can just talk. If it's too loud we can text instead? What's your number?" Jack winked and pulled out his phone.

"Seriously Jack? I'm not as stupid as you sound, please swallow your phone and fuck off!" Sasha smiled and stared him down.

The Old Timer Chase

Prompts: Going through a briar patch
Disclaimer: Hershel and Martha have country accents

Hershel was running full out, but it wasn't very fast. He was old and fat, his running days had long since passed, but on occasion, running was the only option. So much sweat was pouring down his face he felt like he was back in his childhood farm house home, with the shower that had no water pressure. He was huffing so hard it actually distracted him and he tripped over a rock. The fall was the equivalent of a belly flop, off the old Jones Street bridge, into the river. He got up as quickly as he could and stole a look back to see how close his pursuer was, which was a mistake because it only terrified him even more. He got back on his feet and kept running, staring at the ground to avoid any more rocks until he felt something ahead and looked up just in time to run right into a briar patch. Saying it was a patch probably didn't do it justice, it was a wall of brambles. The thorns attacked him, but the one thing Hershel had in his favor was a set of heavy denim overalls and a tough hunting jacket. He forced his way through, but it slowed him down too much. His attacker was on him and it all went to hell.

"I'm tell'n ya, that's what happen'd!" Hershel exclaimed.

"I've been married to you for forty-three years and I don't believe not one word of that!" Martha scrutinized her husband.

"But it's what happen'd! I swear!" Hershel insisted.

"So, you was chased through the back field on the Howard Farm by a three legged black bear wear'n lipstick and it caught you and thas why yer all tossed up, huh?"

143

Martha scrunched up her face into a grimace. "Yer sleep'n in tha barn ta'night!"

Big Goals

Prompts: Words to describe a villain: sneaky, notorious,
skeezy, smart, devious

Fausto looked out his window at the minions
below, going about their various routines. His
underground empire had grown nicely over the decades.

He'd started from the ground up as a low-level
grunt working for a two-bit mafia family, until he realized
that they didn't understand the true meaning of villainy.
Their idea of sneaky was wearing a hat with the brim
pulled low. Not to mention the mafia had some of the
skeeziest people you'd ever meet.

Fausto was looking for smart people. Foot soldiers
with a devious mindset. Once he built up a large enough
group, their network grew and it wasn't long before his
name was notorious enough to garner the respect of the
underworld as well as the law. Even police knew not to
cross him.

He now commanded a small army of highly
motivated criminals who understood the larger scope of
his plans. To run not just one thing, but everything. They
were right now on the edge of running their very first
country. It was a small South American country, but still,
it had taken a lot of work and he was proud. Fausto was
redefining what it meant to be a villain.

Are you Serious?

Prompts: Epic fight

Jennifer stared at Tom. She could feel the blood rushing to her face. It was go time.

"Are you serious Tom?" She ground out through gritted teeth.

"What? Um, yeah I guess so." Tom said, totally caught off guard.

"Don't you brush me off like that!" Jennifer yelled.

"I'm not brushing...uh, what's wrong?" Tom stared at her.

"Playing dumb isn't going to make it go away!" Jennifer grilled him.

"Make what go away? What did I do?" Tom asked as he put the bag of potato chips down on the table.

"I specifically asked you to make dinner tonight. I told you I was gonna be slammed at work and I'd REALLY APPRECIATE some hot food when I got home." Jennifer reminded him.

"Well yeah hun I know, but-" Tom started, but was cut off.

"Don't you 'but me' you lazy asshole. I work all day long so you can stay home and pretend to be an artist and you can't even treat me with some simple decency? What the fuck is wrong with you?" She yelled.

Just then the doorbell rang.

"Who the hell is that? If you are cheating on me with some Instagram slut, we are done!" Jennifer was livid.

"It's not like that Jen, I swear." Tom said nervously.

147

Tom got up answered the door and came back in the room with two bags.

"What the fuck is that?" Jennifer eyed the bags.

"I was trying to tell you, I ordered your favorite sushi place. I couldn't remember which rolls you liked, so I got a bunch." Tom explained.

"Oh..." Jennifer's face dropped. "That was so sweet of you!" She smiled.

What is it?

Prompts: Things pets find interesting but we don't:
bones, licking, sniffing, boxes

Jones stared at Barnaby who had the most insightful looking expression. His head tilted, pointing his ears to one side with an unanswered question.

"Barnaby, what do you want?" Jones asked his Australian Cattle Dog.

Barnaby barked and smacked the ground with both paws.
Jones got up and grabbed a bone from his doggy toy box. He held it up and waved it back and forth, Barnaby's eyes tracked it until Jones threw it and the dog just watched it go flying, then looked back at his owner with the same expectant expression.

"Okay, so not the bone... I don't know buddy... you wanna show me something?" Jones asked.

Barnaby barked, then jumped up.

"Alright, take me to it. C'mon, let's go!" Jones commanded.

Barnaby spun around and began sniffing the ground heading away from the barn, leading to the back garden. Jones walked behind him, more to humor the dog than anything else. Barnaby stopped at a large round rock and began licking it.

"What? It's a rock!" Jones rolled his eyes.

Barnaby barked and pawed at the rock. Sighing, Jones dug out around the rock until he got some purchase and then pulled it up. Underneath was a metal tin with a circus scene from the early 1930's on it. Barnaby went nuts, barking and wagging his tail. Jones dug out the box and opened it up. Inside was a gold pocket watch, some silver dollars from 1894 and an old picture of his farm house with his great grandfather's family standing in front of it, each with their very own horse.

"Ya did good boy." Jones smiled and patted Barnaby on the head.

It's Mine!

Prompts: There's only one left, what do you do?

Ripley's stomach growled as she opened the refrigerator and looked inside for something to eat.

"We got any leftovers?" Kyle asked.

"There's one serving of that homemade pizza from Saturday night." She answered.

"Only one? Hhhmmmm I'll flip ya for it!" Kyle grinned.

"How about I flip you off for it!" Ripley stared at him. "How could you say that?"

"I mean, I'm hungry now." Kyle shrugged his shoulders.

"So, I should go without so you can be satisfied?" Ripley squinted her eyes.

"You can make something else to eat." Kyle smiled.

"Oh, I see. How about this...how about I shove the pizza down your throat in one piece so you can enjoy it ALL AT ONCE!" Ripley yelled.

"Uummm....no...." Kyle stared, "you know what, you can have the pizza, okay?"

"Oh, but then your sensitive tummy would go without! And I'll have to listen to you grumbling all night." Ripley complained.

Kyle moved to the side, opened the cabinet and saw a boxed meal for two. It was one of those add an egg and some meat, heat up on the stove with butter kinda things. He opened it up and started making the meal, even remembering there was some veggie chicken bits in the freezer he could use.

"Yeah, I see what you're doing...I'm still eating the pizza!" She smirked.

151

Late Night Call

Prompts: Annoying things life partners do - get arrested, snore, failing to listen, lie

Tom was jolted awake by his cellphone ringing. He vaguely registered anything but his pillow, it was still dark outside. His dog Chucklehead was snoring loudly at the foot of the bed. The phone continued to ring loudly. He picked it up and saw a strange number.

"Yeah, hello?" Tom answered sleepily.

"Hey sweetie it's me," Nancy giggled with a smile.

"What the hell Nancy, it's 3:47am... why are you calling me?" Tom grimaced.

"Well...I need you to come bail me out...I got arrested." Nancy admitted.

"Arrested? For what?" Tom was now livid and wide awake.

"Well, I can tell you that later, just come get me please." Nancy insisted.

"Naw, unuh, you woke me up, you tell me now." Tom commanded.

"I flashed my boobs at someone and they arrested me." She explained.

"Fine, you wanna lie to me, you can spend the night in jail." Tom stated.

"Okay, Okay...I had a lil tiny bit too much to drink and I was at the bar and I left and I guess I was swerving a bit..." Nancy meandered.

"And you got pulled over?" Tom continued.

"And I hit a cop car." Nancy grimaced.

"You never listen to me...I've told you a hundred times, you shouldn't be riding that damn bicycle to the bar without me!" Tom rolled his eyes.

The Standoff

Prompts: The Worst Possible Experience

Paulie sat in the chair across the table from Tabetha, giving her the stare of death. She was munching loudly on a box of crunchy double chocolate biscotti Italian cookies. She stared back at him the entire time. This had started with her arguing about him leaving the toilet seat up all the time and devolved into a staring contest until she got hungry and decided to taunt him.

"My nona would be sick of you by now." Paulie gritted.

"Oh yeah? I figure she was sick of you the first time ya met." Tabetha raised an eyebrow.

"You know those ain't fresh. My nona make's em fresh just for me." Paulie stated, pointing his thumb at his chest.

"Really? How come I got some now and you don't?" She crunched loudly on a biscotti end.

"Maybe I ate them all so your fat ass couldn't have any!" Paulie snidely answered.

"Yeah? Well I can loose weight for this fat ass, but you still gonna be a stupid ass and ain't no homemade cookies fix'n that shit!" She spat.

"You think I'm stupid huh? You the one who moved in here!" Paulie chuckled.

"Yeah? So what?" She grimaced.

"That makes you stupider!" Paulie pointed out.

"Psssh, that ain't true....stupider ain't a word." She rolled her eyes.

155

Ya Gotta Do It

Prompts: Things you like, that most people don't: opera,
rusty tools, rubber ducks

Jeremy zipped up his overall uniform and snugged the baseball cap on his head. He checked his toolbox and utility belt to make sure everything was in its place. The toolbox had several rusty tools in it, he'd accidentally left in under an air conditioner and the water condensed and dripped inside without him realizing it. He really needed to clean them up, but somehow he had gone on for seven months with the brownish orange tools.

"Hey, you're gonna love it out there today," John called over to him from his locker.

"What? Did someone throw up on stage again?" Jeremy asked with dread.

"There might be some puke in all that mess, it's hard to tell." John smirked.

"Well why didn't you clean it up?" Jeremy eyed him.

"Hey, I was on lightbulbs today. That high pole work takes forever." John raised his hands in defense.

Jeremy sighed, he'd done the light bulbs about six months ago, they were about sixty feet up and with the opera seating in the way, you had to use a very long pole to unscrew them and lower the old bulb to the ground before raising a new replacement up to the same socket. Jeremy hating doing it. He sighed and braced himself for what was coming. He grabbed the cleaning supplies and headed out onto the opera house stage to find it filled with hundreds of rubber ducks of all sizes.

"You gotta be ducking kidding me." Jeremy rolled his eyes.

Trash Talk

Prompts: Things people say, but they shouldn't

Peter opened the front door and stepped inside, immediately running into trash on the floor, which had been pushed up against the door. He forcefully shoved his way in and then kicked stuff out of the way. He set down his briefcase and took off his trench coat.

"This oughta be good." He mumbled under his breath.

Peter made his way through the piles of trash, which apparently populated the entire house. At the very least, the first floor.

"Dolores! Where are you!" Peter yelled.

"Help." Dolores called quietly from the living room.

Peter made his way into the living room and stared at an even bigger mess.

"Are you kidding me? You sit on your fat ass all day long and today you decided to trash the entire house? Literally? This is bullshit. I put up with you pretending to run an unsuccessful business because it kept you busy, but that shit is over now! You're gonna get up and clean this whole damn house! Do you hear me?" Peter ranted.

"Help." Dolores moaned.
Peter walked around the couch and found Dolores tied up on the floor.

"What the fuck happened?" Peter asked as he untied her and sat his wife up against the couch.

"Robbers." Dolores breathed.

"We got robbed? By who?" Peter asked.

"Chip n' dales." Dolores smiled.

"We got robbed by male strippers!" Peter yelled.

The Truth about my Dog

Prompts: If pets were made of fruit

Tommy stared at his dog. His girlfriend Nancy always complained that he had not really tried very hard to give him a good name, but Tommy always thought naming him Concord was rather appropriate. He was made of grapes. Tommy loved Concord grapes and it seemed like the perfect dog to get. Once the grapes were ripe, Tommy either picked them off for a snack, or he'd find them rolling around on the floor. Nancy also thought it was gross that he was eating his dog.

"You know that's not sanitary." Nancy grimaced.

"I wash them, what's wrong with eating his grapes?" Tommy chewed on a juicy one.

"Ugh... you don't wash all of them! I've seen you sneaking them right off his back when he comes over for snuggles on the couch!" Nancy chided him.

"Okay, every once in a while, sure." Tommy admitted.

"I don't see why you couldn't get a normal pet." Nancy shook her head.

"Like what? Dogs are the best." Tommy replied as he popped another grape in his mouth.

"Well, what about some of those fruit rollup lizards?" Nancy suggested. "They stay in a sanitary enclosure."

"Really? That's normal to you?" Tommy side eyed her.

"Okay, um... how about a kiwi kitten." Nancy smiled.

161

"Have you seen what happens when they get ripe? That juice goes everywhere and I'm not cleaning that up!" Tommy shook his head.

"Banana monkey! Who doesn't love bananas?" Nancy yelled.

"Oh okay...I get it now... you hate grapes, huh?" Tommy stared.

Nancy sulked and averted her eyes.

Fussy Feast

Prompts: What are you having for your last supper - pizza, roasted cauliflower, all the sushi, pork ribs, dried seaweed snack, raw liver, red curry with potatoes

Linda sighed heavily and looked at the dinner table. It was the most unexpected and eclectic layout of food yet. She had enjoyed some leftover Sushi from last night, a few spicy tuna rolls, mixed in with eel roles. She really loved the unagi sauce. The rest of the food on the table was laid out in an effort to get Anthony to eat something.

Her mother had insisted on bringing over roasted cauliflower as part of her new health kick. Anthony threw that across the room and it shattered like a white explosion when it hit the floor. He tried the same thing with the dried seaweed snacks, but they were so light the sheets just flipped back around and stuck to his wet face, which then caused him to get flustered and claw at it like bees were attacking him.

She'd offered him red curry with potatoes, a favorite, but he just crossed his arms and shook his head, refusing to eat it.

"Anthony, you need to eat something. What do you want?" Linda asked with tired eyes.

"I want porky!" Anthony yelled.

"We don't have any pork ribs sweetie," Linda grimaced, "how about a peanut butter and jelly sandwich?"

"No! Porky!" Anthony frowned and recrossed his arms.

"I have pizza?" Linda offered.

"No pee zee! Me want Porky!" Anthony yelled.

Linda stared at him, then got up, looked in the fridge and saw a plate of raw liver. It was roughly the same color. She grabbed the plate, cut it up, covered it in BBQ sauce, stuck it in the microwave for two minutes and then brought it to the overly fussy four-year-old who ruled her life.

"Here's your Porky sweetie, I cut it up for you." Linda smiled evilly.

"Thank you mama." Anthony smiled at getting his way, then grabbed a fist full of sauce covered raw liver and stuffed it in his face. He chewed and chewed and chewed, his face looked so confused, but at the same time he didn't want to admit something was wrong.

"You like your pork ribs?" Linda questioned him with needling eyes.

"It's too squeezy mama, make it better." Anthony made a face that equaled what BBQ sauce covered raw liver tasted like.

Something's Wrong

Prompts: You've just returned home

Paul drove down second street, glancing at the fading sunlight as it set early again. He hated the winter time like so many others. He turned right onto Poplar Avenue and then made a quick left into his driveway. He was finally home after an hour-long commute.

Paul grabbed his satchel and headed for the front door, but immediately felt something was wrong. He stopped and looked around. Something definitely wasn't right. He changed directions and swiftly made his way around the house. When he was near the backdoor, he hit the garage remote to open the door. It was very loud and the perfect distraction.

Paul quietly slipped into the house via the backdoor and closed it before anyone could be alerted. Someone was in his house. The automatic lights should be on, but the house was completely dark. His dog didn't great him at the door, nor was he barking. There was definitely something amiss. The backdoor was attached to the kitchen. He opened the pots cabinet and reached under the top to grab the Glock 9mm semi-automatic he kept there for emergencies.

Paul crept forward and stole a glance into the next room by looking at the reflection on his large flatscreen television. Someone was in the room, sitting in his chair. He listened, but didn't hear anyone else in the house. Paul jumped around the wall and pointed the gun at the intruder.

"Lights." Paul called out, which activated all the lighting in the room.

"Hello Paul." The man stared at him, wearing a crisp suit and tie.

"What the hell are you doing in my house?" Paul stared back.

"It's quite simple. I've been trying to contact you about your extended war-" The man was cut off as Paul emptied the clip into the man.

"Fuck your warrantee!" Paul yelled.

Full Day

Prompts: Things small children do - play hopscotch, embarrass their parents, explore fearlessly, poke at things, write on the walls

Timmy ran into the yard as fast as he could and hid behind the large oak tree. His mother burst out the back door with fire in her eyes. It was her Sunday book club meeting and she was all dressed up. The group of women were due to arrive any minute and Timmy had left them a present in the reading room.

"Timothy Herman Johnson! You are in big trouble mister! You get your butt inside right now! I am not going to be embarrassed by your bad behavior in front of my club! You get inside and clean that ridiculous looking book cover off the wall!" His mother yelled.

Timmy of course did not move. He knew this game well and had timed completing his masterpiece just before their arrival so his mother would be more concerned about her friends than about him. She hung in the doorway until the front doorbell chimed and she disappeared back inside.

"Perfectly timed." Timmy chuckled to himself.

He dove between a loose fence board and ran down the street to get Sally. He found her playing hopscotch while bouncing a tennis ball, her own variation on the game.

"Hey, you ready?" Timmy came to a skidding halt.

"Yeah, let's go!" Sally smiled and dropped her ball. They both grabbed their bicycles and pedaled straight into the woods, following a trail they'd been down so many times it was like breathing the fresh mountain air every day. Today however, Timmy took a fork they'd never gone down before and Sally stopped.

167

"What's the matter?" Timmy asked as he stopped and looked back.

"We never been this way before." Sally pointed out.

"Yeah I know...but I heard there's buried treasure down this way." Timmy grinned.

"There is not..." Sally said with her face scrunched up in disbelief.

"Won't know if you don't come find out." Timmy smiled and took off.

Sally watched him go, thought about who would be guarding a buried treasure, then picked up a stick for poking things and also beating up ghosts, then she took off after him.

Mr. Barry

Prompts: Too old for a tantrum

Barry stared out the window and grimaced. It was the same view he saw every day. He was tired of it. Barry grabbed ahold of his cane and used it to knock over all the food containers on his tray to the floor. It made a huge clattering sound, just the way he liked and it got the desired result. Not more than ten seconds had gone by and the quick paced squeaky shoes announced the oncoming arrival of Nurse Carol, who showed up in the doorway with a look on her face that said it all.

"Mr. Barry, did you knock your stuff over again?" Carol asked while staring him down.

"Musta been the wind." Barry smiled with what few teeth he had left.

Carol rolled her eyes and walked into the room to bend over and pick up the cup, plate and other things that had fallen. Unfortunately for Barry, she's gotten wise to his antics and bent over facing him, instead of away, how he liked it. She left the room with all the food containers. He counted out her steps, then used the cane to knock over some books that were directly in front of him which would force her hand. Of course, Carol came hurrying back into the room and looked at the books.

"Earthquake?" Barry raised his eyebrows in confusion.

"I'm gonna quake you Mr. Barry." Carol grumbled.

She got between Barry and the books, bending over the way he liked it, his eyes feasted on her round bottom. She then put the books out of reach of the cane and left the room.

Barry then moved to his backup plan and threw the cane onto the dresser, which knocked over a bunch of noisy items. Carol jumped into the doorway.

"I had a spasm!" Barry complained.

"Ain't nobody got time for this! You are too old to be throwing these tantrums!" Carol steamed.

"But I'm all outta viagra!" Barry complained.

Bad Day

Prompts: Warm Fuzzy Love

Viola closed the door to her apartment and sighed heavily. She dropped her drippy bag on the floor, along with her overly wet wool coat. There had been no mention of rain in the forecast, which was why she decided to walk to the office. That granted her a slogging walk back home through the worst downpour this year. She should have just called a taxi, but her budget was too tight for such frivolous spending. She gazed with tired eyes into her living room at the mess and remembered thinking she would clean it later, but now was later and she was dripping wet. She was drenched to the bone, as her mother loved to say. Viola was no stranger to being caught in the rain, it had been happening since she was a small child. Almost like a curse of some kind. A dryness curse, she thought. Traipsing forward into the room, she gave up and slumped into the couch. The day had beaten her into submission.

Off in the distance, a light chittering chirp announced Francine had risen from her sleeping position. Viola could hear her skittering down the hardwood floor hallway from the bedroom. Suddenly, the large tiger striped tabby appeared next to her head, having leapt from the floor to the back of the couch. She head-bumped Viola, then carefully snaked her way down onto the couch, transitioning slyly she snuggled into Viola's lap, warming off her owners murky chill and made little cute sounds.

"I love you too." Viola smiled and petted Francine's head, then scratched behind her ears.

Home Early

Prompts: When someone finds out you've been naughty -
shy, remorse, oopsie, turned on

Harry opened the door and caught Lisa in the act. He wasn't sure exactly what act it was, but the scene gave rise to many questions. Lisa was naked in the living room, partially covered in peanut butter, but there were scattered brightly colored papers all over the floor. As soon as Lisa saw him, she immediately became shy and attempted to cover up, but couldn't grab anything because her hands had just been smearing Jiffy smooth and creamy over her butt, so she couldn't grab anything without getting it covered in the tasty substance. She instead covered her privates quickly with her hands and arms.

"Um, what exactly is going on here?" Harry asked as he close the door. "Is that my stuff all over the floor?"

"Well I umm...oopsie!" Lisa nervously giggled. "You weren't supposed to see this, I um...sorta." She bit her lip and couldn't finish.

"You seem to have no remorse whatsoever! These are my comics! Why are they torn up!" Harry demanded.

"Okay, Okay, they just look like yours. I went and bought some new old ones that looked like yours and I was gonna, sorta wallpaper myself with the torn pages for you to peel off," Lisa smiled deviously, "you know....with yer teeth."

Harry's demeanor immediately shifted; it was obvious he was now turned on.

"I see, well...let me go get the grape jelly." Harry winked.

Tonight's the Night

Prompts: I didn't like it then, but I love it now.

Frank smiled as he walked down the street and turned the corner to see Kelly's house. They'd been dating for a few months, but it felt like tonight was the night. He was almost giddy with the thought of what was going to happen. He arrived at the front door and rang the doorbell. It seemed like before his finger had even left the button, the door sprang open and there was Kelly with a devious grin on her face. She swayed a little from side to side and invited him in with a nod of her chin.

Once inside, Frank produced the bouquet of flowers he'd been hiding and gave them to Kelly. Her eyes got wide, she grabbed them and then quickly, almost tossed them onto a table before she latched onto Frank. They were so lip-locked the two were breathing each other's air to survive. They stumbled to the couch and fell onto it.

"Tell me what you want," Frank gasped.

This caused Kelly to stop and blush a little bit.

"Well...I hated it when...I used to be bad....um," She bit her lower lip, " Spank me...hard!"

The Garden Happening

Prompts: When Pixies Attack, what do to?

Hellen ran frantically through her garden, dodging the attacks of darting pixies. This was the first time they'd gotten aggressive. She'd always seen them in her garden, sitting on the flowers or washing up with the morning dew, but they'd always been at a distance. Of course, she thought they were cute and a great part of the outdoor atmosphere, but now they were flitting about with such velocity, Hellen felt like she was dodging winged bullets. After circling all over the yard, she finally made it to the garden shed and closed the door just as a pixie smashed into the window and let loose a bunch of squeaky curses which Hellen couldn't make out.

Breathing heavily, Hellen steadied herself and looked around the shed to see what she could use to defend herself. She couldn't stay in there all night, and it was only mid-afternoon, who knew how long they would be out there waiting. Pixies didn't seem like patient things, but maybe they were plotters...revenge? Creatures that plot could wait a long time to enact their plans. Hellen formed her own plan and grabbed some supplies, then cracked open the door a tiny bit before opening it with her foot and rushing out.

She emerged with a metal garbage can lid in one hand, using it as a shield and a badminton racquet in the other. The first pixie to dart at her, was blue and gold. Hellen swatted it into a bush and then quickly blocked a purple and green pixie with her shield as she carefully made her way forward to the house. Her progress was steady and she was succeeding, right until she reached her deck and had to turn around to open the sliding glass door. It was then that she found out, there was a toad the size of a large dog inside her house. It leapt forward and knocked her down. Then a hoard of pixies put twigs, fresh flowers and caterpillars in her hair, laughed hysterically and flew away.

The Double Dog Deal

Prompts: How it feels when doing something you don't
want to do - avoid it, annoying, grumpy

Jason stared at the mess in front of him and
sighed. His wife had insisted on getting two dogs. She also
made it clear they weren't to be crated at any time because
that was mean. He'd voiced his thoughts, but she flatly
ignored him, insisting he just didn't understand dogs. It
was true Jason hadn't had a dog before, but he didn't feel
that invalidated his opinions.

Both dogs were now staring at him, in the center of
what used to be the living room. It was now completely
trashed. They had ripped up the couch, stuffing was
everywhere, the coffee table had been knocked over and
the glass broken. the flatscreen television was on the floor,
bent at a bad angle. The shelving unit with all their
pictures and little knickknacks was broken apart and
trampled. He was extremely annoyed and really wanted to
avoid dealing with it entirely. Why should he have to clean
this up? It was clearly his wife's responsibility. She wanted
the dogs, she was the one who knew so much about them,
she should do it.

Jason stopped himself mid-thought, had he turned
into a grumpy old man? Was this what he'd become?
Jason stared at the dogs who were eagerly awaiting his
attention. Maybe even a treat for a job well done, right?

"You guys did such a great job! Thanks for
everything, I'm sure your mother will be very happy when
she gets home!" Jason said to them in the most sarcastic
voice he could muster.

He promptly turned around, left the house and got
in his truck. He drove down the street to the strip mall
and parked, then pulled out his phone and texted his wife.

'Stopped at the grocery store to pick up some things we need, I'll be a bit late, get dinner started without me.' He smiled to himself and got out of the truck, headed for the store. He's successfully outsmarted his wife and avoided an argument as well. Ten minutes later he got a text from his wife which read: 'You bastard, I know you saw what the dogs did, you are cleaning this shit up when you get home.'

Death By Squirrel

Prompts: How Many Times Is Enough?

Toby trudged up the hill, his backpack was heavy with junk and the wagon behind him was full of wood for the fireplace. A successful outing to be sure, but tiring none-the-less. As he crested the ridge, his house came into view. The smile of relief grew on his face and he quickened up the last little bit of the journey to the log cabin he'd built with Stevie.

Toby opened the front door and there was his wife, dressed like a little Dutch girl. She turned and smiled at him, then frowned a bit.

"What's wrong?" Toby asked.

"The squirrels are back." Stevie answered with dread.

"Again? How many times are these little thieves…" Toby stopped himself as the frustration built up.

He grabbed his shotgun and headed out the door. As if they knew what time he'd be back and wanted to get his reaction, all four squirrels were outside on a stump, chittering away when he exited the cabin. They immediately scattered as Toby took aim with the shotgun, but held his fire. It was only filled with rock salt, but it would still get the message across. Toby grimaced and watched as they all scurried up a large oak tree. He walked over to the base and stared up at them as they ran around the tree.

"Okay, that's fine. You wanna steal from me? Now you pay!" Toby yelled.

He swiftly ran over to the shed and put down his shotgun in favor of the chainsaw. He took a good look at the tree and then figured which direction was the best to fell it. He cut a relief on the back and then went to work on the front. Just before he was about to finish, the chainsaw ran out of gas and also got stuck. He went back to the shed where he kept the wedges and was immediately attacked by all four squirrels.

Just in Time

Prompts: Surprise it's time to _____ : Die, awaken the
inner beast, Do it.

Harry ran full out down the street, feeling his hot
breath washing over his cold cheeks. Winters weren't his
favorite time of year for this very reason. The wind kicked
up and stung his face, forcing his eyes to squint and then a
sudden rapid reintroduction to the ground presented
itself. Harry fell hard as the patch of ice beneath the snow
stole all his power. The impact of the event, combined
with the cold made him feel like he was about to die.

"You're not dying...just get up Harry...get up...DO
IT!" Harry argued with himself.

He forced his way back to a standing position, his
body full of pains and tinges of death. He staggered
forward, thinking about his woman waiting for him, on
the floor, tied up, probably crying. He didn't have much
time. Stagger, skip, step, move. He built up some
momentum as his inner beast awoke and he began to run
again. It wouldn't be long now. He could do it. His house
was in sight. Harry stubbled across the yard, pushed in the
door and pulled the pistol out of his jacket pocket.

"Surprise, you're too late Harry," a mans voice said.

Harry spun around to see a short man in a trench
coat, which was very out of place for several reasons.

"What do you mean too late?" Harry pressed as he
leveled the revolver at the man's head.

"She's gone. Long gone. You blew it." The man spat
out, then turned and walked out of the house.

That Poor Raccoon

Prompts: Don't force me to be nice, always waiting for
the sun to set

Spencer dangled his feet over the edge of the porch, looking out at the horizon. Birds were flitting about, a few squirrels were racing around the yard and a raccoon was desperately trying to escape Spencer's in-ground pool, which made him smile. It wouldn't be long now, Spencer thought to himself.

Lucia walked outside and sat down next to him, which immediately put up his guard. He purposefully didn't greet her.

"Are you doing this again?" Lucia asked snidely.

"I don't know what you mean." Spencer answered, still looking at the horizon.

"You are acting like a dick." Lucia pointed out.

"I'm just waiting for the sun to set." He stated.

"And you can't look at me for even a second to acknowledge   my presence?" She stared at the side of his head.

"Don't force me to be nice Lucia, it's not going to get you anything." Spencer said through gritted teeth.

"Nice? Nice would be an act of God at this point, I'd settle for cordial or polite... why do you have to get like this? It's really annoying you know." Lucia stated then stopped looking at him and decided to focus on the raccoon who was still trying to escape the pool. "That stupid bastard in the pool is nicer to me that you are."

"Lucia... you..." Spencer stopped speaking, took a slow breath in, then stared at her with one eye, "you didn't even apologize."

"For what?" She stared at him.

185

"For what? For crashing my Lamborghini!" Spencer yelled.

"I was asleep! It wasn't my fault!" Lucia yelled back.

"SLEEP DRIVING ISN'T REAL!" Spencer yelled louder.

"I'm so sick and tired of you not believing me." Lucia folded her arms and turned away from him.

"I'm so sorry, it's hard to believe all of your lies, the smaller ones are a bit easier, but you knew how much that car meant to me, it was my fathers and you destroyed it." Spencer stated.

"Oh my god, why are you such a drama queen?" Lucia mumbled.

Spencer swiftly jumped to his feet, picked Lucia up off the porch and threw her into the pool, which created a giant splash that flung the raccoon onto the paved edge around the pool. The raccoon shook himself off, looked at Lucia, chittered his thanks, then ran away.

The Hike

Prompts: Outside and something unexpected happens -
Landscaper, wild rabbit

Bobby was hot and sweaty, but with a bit of a smirk on his face. He'd been planning this hike for weeks. He was admittedly out of shape, but he was committed to hitting his eight-mile goal. The trail was in a national park, but it wasn't one that a lot of people used, which was exactly the reason he'd chosen it. He didn't want to be distracted by any wacky rando's high on pine needles. Something darted across the path.

"Did you see that?" Mary exclaimed.

"I saw something." Bobby mumbled to his wife.

The two stopped walking and scanned the undergrowth. Another burst of speed revealed a white and brown, wild rabbit running down a grade and then disappearing into its hole.

"I don't think I've ever seen a real rabbit hole." Bobby said.

"You do seem to have a problem finding holes." Mary smirked.

"Hey! That was just once! I was drunk!" Bobby blabbered in defense.

"Sure, sure...it was the Budweiser." Mary smiled and nodded her head.

Just then they heard a loud sound, like a tree falling. It was directly in front of them down the path. They both headed quickly toward the sound and found something completely unexpected. There before them in the middle of a national park, was a landscaper, organizing a large garden area. It was complete with bush statues and log benches. Upon seeing them he waved. They walked over to the center of the area and approached him.

187

"What are you doing?" Bobby asked.

"Watchu mean? I'm make'n it look nice." Hector Smiled.

Springtime Walk

Prompts: I had no idea those grew back!

Melissa walked her dog Fergie down the street on a nice Spring afternoon. It was still cool enough to wear a light jacket in the mountains of Pennsylvania. She smiled at the familiar faces she saw each day, but didn't know the names which belonged to them. Most people really liked Fergie, so she'd had plenty of interaction with the neighborhood people who liked to be outside. As she rounded the corner, they approached Mr. Mcfaddons house. He was outside working in the garden with his overalls and straw hat. He stood up and waved as they got closer, which meant he had a dog treat for Fergie.

Melissa walked right into the garden area which was full of flowers and vegetables. It looked like a much better version of her own garden. Just then she saw Berty the tabby cat on Mr. McFaddon's porch, swatting her tail back and forth.

"I got a treat for someone!" Mr. McFaddon called out as Fergie lunged forward to get his biscuit.

"Um, Mr. McFaddon...is that...the same cat?" Melissa asked oddly.

"Oh uh, yeah...that's Berty. Don't you recognize her?" He asked.

"Well yeah, but didn't she...her tail got run over last Fall and it was amputated wasn't it?" Melissa stared.

"Oh yeah... it grew back."

"What? I had no idea those grew back!" Melissa said in a shock filled voice.

"Apparently neither did Berty, she keeps attack'n that tail like it was made by the devil!" Mr. McFaddon announced.

As if on cue, Berty attacked her tail with ferocity, rolling back and forth until she fell right off the side of the porch into the bushes.

You know Who to Blame

Prompts: Oh My God, it's you.

Dirk was beat down from a full day of work. He hated the office, but it was the only job he could get in the current crappy economy, thanks to the lack of government planning. At least, that's what he told himself. It was also the reason his wife had left him. He hadn't been making enough money for her, so she found a richer man to buy her things. They weren't even divorced. Who had money for a divorce lawyer these days? Dirk slotted the house key in the front door and went inside. Entering the living room, he stopped short.

"Oh my god...Olivia?" Dirk stared.

There on his couch, wearing lacy black lingerie and nothing else, was his ex-girlfriend from eight years ago.

"I heard that bitch was off boning some rich pecker....I thought you might be....a little lonely." Olivia smiled suggestively at him.

"Well, um...yeah that's true...but...how did you get in?" Dirk was still in shock.

"Remember when I gave you your key back when we broke up? Well...I made a copy. I always figured I was gonna come by when you weren't home and move stuff around like the house was haunted....but then I dated this huge asshole and once I finally got away from him, I realized that you were the man for me." Olivia explained.

"So, you've just been here...half naked...waiting for me?" He stared at her body.

"Of course not....I also made dinner." Olivia replied, which immediately brought the smell of parmigiana chicken to his nose.

"So get over here before the food gets cold." Olivia winked at him.

Artsy Surprise

Prompts: Of course, I know how to paint that - a wall,
brightly colored

Wearing her overly fluffy robe, Jessie took deep strides into the room and looked at Micky who had laid out a bunch of art supplies on the living room table.

"Are you ready?" Jessie smirked.

"As ready as I can be, you didn't really give me much to go on." Micky replied, staring at her robe and pointing, "Why are you in your robe?"

Jessie dropped her robe to the floor and revealed that she was naked, with instructions. There was a paper taped to her waist that was covering her bikini region. All over her body was black magic marker lines which sectioned her off into a design of sorts. Each area was labeled with a number. Micky stared at the her, then at the paper which pointed out what he was supposed to do. He jumped up and snatched the paper off her, which made her jump and jiggle a bit with a smile.

"I thought you wanted to paint a wall or something." Micky half looked at the paper, but mainly stared at her body.

"Oh, well if you prefer the wall-" Jessie started.

"No-no, that wall doesn't exist anymore." Micky cut her off.

"Make sure you use the fluorescent paints, I want to be brightly colored." Jessie said and she used her hands to display certain body areas.

"And what happens if I paint outside the lines?" Micky asked.

"Oh…if you're naughty? Then you might not get the present I have for you…in the kitchen." Jessie taunted him.

"The kitchen huh?" Micky tried to look over her shoulder.

"No-no naughty boy, you finish your meal before you get dessert." Jessie said. Then she jumped on top of him and rode him to the floor lip-locked.

The Revelation

Prompts: That stain is never coming out.

Nathan opened his eyes and felt disoriented. He was on the ground, flat on his back. Where he was and how he got there was a mystery. Sitting up, Nathan looked around at the gloomy wooded area, which seemed unusually dark despite the sun glaring down from directly over his head. Getting to his feet, he immediately lost his balance and lurched forward, trying to steady himself. It felt like a giant weight was on his chest, pulling him back to the ground. It was too heavy, like a thick steel plate attached to his torso. Nathan lifted up his shirt and found a black mark going from his belly button up to cover his chest.

"What...why do I have this?" Nathan was confused. He touched the mark and it was ice cold.

"That stain will never come off." Jobellz stated.

Nathan swung around quickly towards the voice and immediately lost whatever balance he had, then involuntarily kissed the ground. He pushed up on one arm to look at the creature standing above him. It was humanoid, furry in parts and had horns. It too was black like his mark, but all over its entire body.

"What the hell are you?" Nathan asked.

"I am a cursed stain." Jobellz replied.

"A what? How do you know this black thing isn't coming off me?" Nathan breathed heavily, the exertion to speak was tiring him out.

"I know....because that's how my stain started out...two hundred years ago."

No He Didn't

Prompts: You should never ever BBQ that.

Larry walked outside in his Hawaiian shirt, straw hat and swimming trunks, with a large platter of chicken wings covered in his special blend of seasoning. He'd started up the grill about thirty minutes ago, hoping it would be ready just in time. His eyes nearly shot out of his head as he saw his eight-year-old son Bert. The boy had pulled a storage bin over to the cooker, opened it up and was throwing his outdoor plastic toys into it.

Larry quickly put down the platter, ran over and grabbed the tongs, yanking out all the toys before they melted or caught fire. Once the last one was out, he looked at Bert, who was confused.

"Bert, you should never BBQ your toys." Larry stated.

"But...won't they taste better?" Bert asked.

"No! They won't! Toy's ain't for eat'n son!" Larry chastised him.

"But I'm hungry papa." Bert complained.

It should be noted that Bert was about three feet tall and a hundred eighty pounds. The phrase butter-ball always came to mind when looking at him.

"Son, ya only eat stuff that's for eat'n. Do you see that plate of wangs I brought out?" Larry pointed.

"I done didn't see it before now..." Bert stared.

"Pick up all these toys off the patio and put them away." Larry commanded.

"Aww man, do I gotta pa?" Bert whined.

"Do you want some these wangs?" Larry pointed out.

"Well 'course I want'em." Bert mumbled.

197

"Git ta pick'n boy!" Larry grumbled and picked up the platter of chicken.

"Aw fudge nuts." Bert fussed and began kicking his half-melted toys off the patio.

The Run

Prompt: Noob Identified – Clumsy, mistake, launch, roll

Fava's run looked like one leg was shorter than the other by several inches, it was more of a controlled hobble that was constantly on the verge of becoming a tumble and roll. Sweat was running profusely down his chubby face and his breathing was labored. To say his lack of preparation was a mistake would be like saying he shouldn't have had that third helping of cookies...Fava was a chronic procrastinator.

He rounded the corner on his bad leg and hit a patch of loose gravel, which launched him sideways into the alley wall. He rebounded off, hopped back the other way, spun around and managed to stay on his feet. A woman down the other end of the alley had seen the entire thing, he felt embarrassed and clumsy, but there was nothing to be done about it now. He started running again until he got to the side door in the alley and hefted it open to dive inside. Stomping his way up the stairs, he made it to the second floor and knocked loudly on a door. It opened suddenly.

"Well, look who decided to show up," Charlie grimaced.

"Yeah sorry!" Fava breathed.

"Noob identified!" Karl yelled from the other room, "Get in here already, we play two games without you!"

Fava huffed and trudged inside with a smile on his face.

The Process

Prompt: Killing Spree – Unexpected, ridiculous, red-eyed, angry

Susan stood outside with her eyes closed, standing perfectly still. To an outside observer, she could have been a well-painted statue, save for the rustle of her clothing in the breeze. While the unexpected wind felt nice against her skin, it did nothing to calm her angry mind, which was an endless looped rage filled scenario.

The bank tower clock struck noon and her lids popped open, revealing her red-eyed stare of ill intent. Someone passed in front of her to get in the front door, but Susan was in no mood to have someone else set her pace. She grabbed the man be the scruff of his neck, smashed his face into the door then let him drop to the ground as she went inside.

The security guard spotted her right off, but she wasn't having it, Susan closed the distance rapidly, and punched him in the throat. His ridiculous attempt to unholster his gun was pointless as she grabbed it while he fell to the floor. Susan shot him in the head, then spun the gun on the nearest person, head shot.

Screaming erupted all around her, she threw her bag inside, pulling the ignition cord in the process and waited for the grenades to explode while she took cover behind a half wall. The killing spree had begun. They'd be sorry, real sorry they didn't approve her car loan.

The Apple

Prompt: Ghost – translucent, wispy, luscious, organic

Lilly tossed an apple into her lunch bag and stopped to stare at it. Was that the organic apple she bought for lunch or the cheap apple she was going to feed to Kelly, her horse. The pause seemed to go on for too long and she couldn't recall which one it was, so she went back to the fridge to get another apple, only to find there were no more in the crisper drawer.

"Are you serious Lilly? You're debating apples and there was only one all along?" She mumbled under her breath.

"Sorry, I took the other apple," A voice behind her responded.

Lilly spun around to see a ghost on the other side of her kitchen island. It was a man, dressed in clothing from the 1970's, brightly colored, but muted due to his body's translucent appearance. Something was wrong with his hair too, it was all wispy, like he was stuck in some slow-motion wind or underwater.

"Look, um... what are you doing in my kitchen?" Lilly stared, unable to think what else to say. "Did you just say you took my other apple?"

"Yeah, sorry I didn't ask, it was a luscious red color and my wife did love apples..." He said.

"But you can't even eat apples!" Lilly demanded.

"How would you know? You've never been a ghost before." The man said matter-of-factly, as he grabbed the apple out of her bag and ate that one too.

The Question

Prompt: Boogey Man – silent, glowing, dark, terrifying

Gustav sat in the highbacked leather chair and swallowed with difficulty, trying his best to remain still in the mostly dark room. Lars stood in front of him, flexing the tight leather gloves on his hands, making the leather creak with strain. The sound was unnerving.

"Where is it?" Lars asked.

"I-I-don't know," Gustav stammered.

Lars punched him in the face so hard the chair rocked back and nearly tipped over, but teetered forward at the last moment, nearly ejecting him to the floor. Gustav's vision was hazy and glowing, the little bits of light in the room seemed way too bright for the darkness that surrounded him.

"Tell me!" Lars yelled.

Gustav barely had time to lock his eyes onto the sound as the closet door burst open, and the boogey man lumbered out of the shadows, his terrifying presence nearly causing a heart attack. Lars spun around toward the monster only to be caught by the throat. The boogey man pulled him in close, his face mere millimeters away.

"I've been trying to reach you...about your...problem...being an asshole." The boogey man dredged, then snapped Lars's neck and disappeared back into the closet.

Raised in Morristown, New Jersey, P. J. started his story telling by drawing comics with his younger brother Anthony while they were children. Continuing on to college, poetry took hold for a while, along with more than a few short stories. In the late 1990's an idea for a screenplay was born and later realized in the early 2000's, **My Soul to Keep,** his first feature length piece, a children's fantasy film. This led P. J. to film school at the New York Film Academy in 2007. Graduating in 2008, he worked full time in the film industry while also writing dozens of short films and several feature films. Later on in 2015, he completed his first novel, **The Legend of La La Land**, which is yet unpublished. The poetry bug was also reignited following the book, with over four hundred poems posted on Instagram. His passion for story telling stems from an overly active imagination, vividly lucid dreams at night and a fearless mindset. P. J. has plans for an entire series based on **The Legend of La La Land.**

www.ingramcontent.com/pod-product-compliance
Lightning Source LLC
Chambersburg PA
CBHW061146170626
46809CB00003B/1001